SHAMBLER

SHAMBLER

An Insider's Novel
of the Comic Book World

Michael L. Fleisher

iUniverse, Inc.

New York Lincoln Shanghai

SHAMBLER

An Insider's Novel of the Comic Book World

iUniverse books may be ordered through booksellers or by contacting:

iUniverse
2021 Pine Lake Road, Suite 100
Lincoln, NE 68512
www.iuniverse.com
1-800-Authors (1-800-288-4677)

Because of the dynamic nature of the Internet, any Web addresses
or links contained in this book may have changed
since publication and may no longer be valid.

This is a work of fiction. All of the characters, names, incidents, organizations, and
dialogue in this novel are either the products of the author's imagination or are used
fictitiously.

ISBN: 978-0-595-48071-5 (pbk)
ISBN: 978-0-595-60170-7 (ebk)

Printed in the United States of America

CHAPTER 1

▼

"I've never done this before," stammered Kevin. "What do we do?"

"You can jerk off, okay?" she replied. "And I'll take my clothes off."

Only seconds before, Kevin had sucked in his breath and dropped a heavy hexagonal token into the coin slot. It had fallen home with a portentous thunk, and then the lights inside the booth had blinked out and the opaque black screen behind the transparent plexiglass wall panel had begun its ascent. Only at the last instant had it occurred to Kevin to snatch the telephone receiver from its cradle and nestle it securely against his ear.

"I don't think I want to jerk off. Could we talk a little?"

"Sure, why not?"

Kevin could see her clearly through the plexiglass, facing him from within a starkly lit booth that was the virtually identical counterpart of his.

"Whatta you wanta talk about?" she asked him.

"I don't know."

"Okay, then what's your name?"

She was slender and petite, about five-foot-three, with small, firm breasts and curly peroxide-blond hair. Her golden-yellow terrycloth bikini evoked her hair color, and her long, graceful fingernails had been polished a luscious, liquid crimson to match her lips.

"Kevin," he answered.

"Where you from, Kevin?"

"New York."

"A native New Yorker?"

"Sort of, I guess so."

"And you've never been here before?"

He paused. "Here, yes, but not to a booth."

"How come?"

"I—I don't know. I guess—"

Without warning, the opaque black screen descended—shutting off the view through the plexiglass—and the lights inside Kevin's booth blinked on. Kevin hurriedly dug out his second token and thrust it urgently into the slot. Once again, the booth went dark. Once again, the offending panel rose.

"Whatta you do for a living, Kevin? You got a job?"

"I write comic books."

"You draw—"

"No. Write them. I write the scripts. Somebody else—"

"Are you gonna put this place into one of your stories? And you've never been to a booth before, right?"

Kevin shook his head.

"Whatta you think of it?"

He shrugged.

"Look, if you decide to jerk off—"

Once again, the black screen descended and the lights winked on. Kevin was out of tokens and, at two dollars a pop, not at all certain that he wanted to buy more. The floor was slippery, slick with the too-hastily sponge-mopped semen of the patrons who'd occupied this booth before him. All of a sudden, Kevin began to feel queasy. He undid the latch and ran out the door.

CHAPTER 2

▼

The Indy Con was strictly small potatoes, and Kevin had even had to pay for his own hotel room and plane fare now that those morons at Dynamic Comics had bumped him off their preferred list. They were pissed at him for being so late with the Silver Cicada, but Kevin was confident they'd warm up to him again once they actually saw it. Still, showing the flag at these conventions was important, even at the small ones, because reporters from the fan press were always there, along with the local distributors and retailers, and sometimes you could even uncover some hot new artistic talent before writers from both the major companies—Dynamic Comics and Majestic Comics—began swarming all over him. The way the business was evolving these days, it was the writers who spotted and teamed up with the new guys who really stood to make the bucks.

He still had an hour to kill before his panel, so he meandered around the dealers' room, making small talk with the dealers, shaking his head sympathetically when they complained about how the rampant speculation in hot new titles had all but obliterated the once-thriving market in rare old back issues, and how a guy could practically retire now if only he'd had the foresight to order more heavily on *Grim Gladiator* #1. Occasionally, Kevin would pick up a few old titles on his rounds to fill in the blanks in his own collection, but he'd begun doing less and less of that these days now that he was working less and money was short. Now and then, one of the fans would come up to him and ask him to autograph an old back issue of *The Shambler*, but they tended to be the older fans, in their early-to-mid-thirties, like Kevin. The Shambler's thirty-four-issue run had ended some seven years previously, and Kevin hadn't really enjoyed a critical or commercial success since then. A lot of the younger kids, it seemed, didn't even recognize him—maybe they didn't even know his name, although to Kevin that notion seemed pretty far-fetched. All that would change, of course, once they saw the Cicada. Assuming, that is, he ever finished the damn thing. It had all gotten so damned impossible since the onset of his writer's block.

At the booths of the small, independent companies, each of which published a meager three or four titles a month, Kevin cordially smiled and shook hands with the publishers, reconfirming old contacts and initiating new ones. One never knew what the world held in store: if the day ever came when he was bounced by Dynamic Comics, these were the guys he'd have to work for.

Glancing around the huge velour-draped ballroom, Kevin spied a slew of familiar New York faces, all of them flown out here to the boonies to pimp their stuff. Guido Gallante was there, probably pimping for real. The way he hacked out his artwork, it was no wonder that the main way he got work was by providing a steady stream of women to Majestic's editor-in-chief. Gallante also lent money to people, at usurious rates, and there was even a rumor that Gallante had mob connections, even though nobody knew for certain if it was really true.

Ed Scanlon was on hand, too, looking all rheumy-eyed and penitent from his latest hangover. Age 40, but looking every inch fifty-five, Scanlon had pencilled some classic Lightning Lord stories about fifteen years ago, when his kind of puerile, cartoony style was still in, but today he'd be scrabbling for handouts in Grand Central Station if Octavia weren't tossing him the occasional fill-in.

Over in a corner of the giant room, safely clear of the convention-going throng, Freddy Minsk and Sol Bernstein protectively straddled their giant portfolios while briskly swapping triple-X-rated videotapes. Minsk had cleaned up last year with his seamy Spectral Avenger revival series, and it had become something of an industry pastime to try to identify the sundry porn stars on whom he'd modeled his characters.

Kevin exited the dealers' room and wandered along a hotel corridor in search of a men's room. The plush carpeting was characterized by an optically disconcerting, jigsaw-puzzle-like pattern in royal blue and white, and Kevin found himself all but compelled to raise his eyes to avoid it, even though he'd grown accustomed to looking down when he walked to deemphasize what small vestiges remained of the scars on his face. Then, all at once, a set of double doors at the other end of the hallway swung open, and a gaggle of mostly teenaged fans, clad in homemade costumes modeled after those worn by their favorite comic-book characters, surged toward him and then past him down the hall. A stunning young brunette, fetchingly attired in the black leather minidress and hip-high boots of the Black Spider, led the pack, protectively clutching the costume contest's coveted first-prize trophy to her breast. Kevin looked to see whether any of the contestants had come as the Shambler, or even the Golden Starling, but, to his momentary disappointment, none of them had.

Proceeding briskly down the white-and-gold-toned corridor, past the wide-open doorway of the Dynamic Comics hospitality suite, Kevin caught a fleeting glimpse of George Pfister, the creator of Power Man, who had at long last enacted a brittle truce with Dynamic after nearly forty bitter litigious years. Of course the old man was completely blind now—he'd long since been forced to resign, due to disability, his job as a file clerk with the Social Security Administration— but there he sat, surrounded by well-wishers, scratching out crude sketches of Power Man with an ancient Rapidograph and autographing them for respectful fans.

If not for Power Man, there would have been no comics industry, which meant that every fan, pro, and retailer owed George Pfister an incalculable debt. As a high-school boy in Decatur, Illinois, in 1936, Pfister had created Power Man—the world's first superhero—in a burst of predawn inspiration after seeing a flying, bulletproof man in a dream. He had sold his creation to Dynamic Magazines, Inc.—eventually to become Dynamic Comics—for a hundred and twenty-five dollars outright, and although he had made a comfortable living for the better part of a decade writing and drawing the earliest Power Man stories, when his eyesight began to deteriorate in the mid-1940s, and Pfister could no longer keep up with his deadlines, the company fired him, cutting him off without a cent. Pfister responded by suing Dynamic to regain his copyright, only to lose repeatedly in court after court. Finally, old, sightless, and nearly destitute, Pfister had resorted to mass-mailing a nut letter to the nation's media, threatening to jump off the World Trade Center in a Power Man costume on Power Man's fiftieth birthday unless Dynamic relented and entered into some kind of settlement. Now here he was, ensconced like a decrepit old lapdog in Dynamic's hospitality suite, staring sightlessly at his sketch pad and scrawling pathetically in exchange for lifelong medical benefits and a measly twenty thousand a year.

"Hi there, Kev!"

Kevin whirled, and found himself standing face to face with Sol Bernstein.

"I thought I spotted you in there," exclaimed Sol. "What the hell brings you way out here?"

"Oh, the usual, I suppose," replied Kevin. "I'm on a panel. It starts, as a matter of fact, in less than—"

"How's Eugènie?" persisted Bernstein. "I hear you and she—"

"She's fine," answered Kevin abruptly, "thanks."

"And how about the Cicada, Kev? When are we—"

"Soon," stammered Kevin. "Soon. And it's going to be great."

"Any chance of my getting an advance—"

"No," replied Kevin.

"I just scored some great Vera Hale shit from Freddy Minsk, Kev," continued Bernstein, dipping into the oversized portfolio between his knees. "Would you like—"

"Not now," answered Kevin. "I can't. The panel. Maybe later. I'm in 439." And with that he turned on his heel and sped away.

Bernstein was a brilliant colorist, and he had accumulated what was undoubtedly the finest Vera Hale collection in the entire United States. An anonymous nude calendar model during World War II, Hale had achieved a kind of tawdry stardom by posing—shackled, bound, gagged, and harnessed—for such hard-core bondage magazines as *Bizarre Bondage* and *Daring Discipline* before vanishing mysteriously from public view at the onset of the 1950s. Now in her sixties and presumed to be living in retirement under either an assumed or married name, she had become the revered object of a small but devoted cult dedicated to amassing her quite substantial oeuvre and, if at all possible, divining her whereabouts, so that she could be brought forward to receive the homage she deserved.

Kevin barely arrived on time for his panel. Like most such pretentious events of its kind, this one—titled "Transfiguration and Death in the American Comic Book"—was an object lesson in boredom, and it frankly nettled Kevin that nearly all the questions were directed at the other guests. Two questioners, however, asked him about the Silver Cicada, and Kevin tried hard to be as tantalizing as possible without conveying any actual news.

It was nearly midnight by the time he returned to his hotel room. Digging deep into his luggage for his can of Lysol disinfectant spray, he carried it into the bathroom and carefully coated every surface with a fine Lysol mist. Then he laid out the contents of his toiletry kit and began painstakingly flossing his teeth. A half-hour later he lay sprawled on his bed, absentmindedly watching late-night TV. The hotel had a closed-circuit adult channel, but all it showed was ancient black-and-white footage of big-breasted bimbos at nudist camps, sprawled over beach balls and hitting a volleyball over a net. After about twenty minutes of that nonsense, he turned out the lights and went to sleep.

CHAPTER 3

▼

"… wanted to mail them out to you, certified, but I said no, you were coming out here anyway, I said I'd rather just hand them to you myself. It seems more human somehow. And besides, I hate certified."

She had just finished pouring herself a mugful of Nestle's International Coffees Orange-Mocha Cappuccino Instant, and now she was dropping in the sugar cubes with the monotonous regularity of a ticking clock—four cubes, five cubes, six cubes, seven. It made Kevin nauseous to watch her do it, but he always watched and counted along silently with her anyway, like an anthropologist bearing witness to some particularly gruesome yet spellbinding rite.

They were seated in the breakfast nook of the Roslyn, Long Island, home they'd shared for three years until Kevin had moved out, just under six months ago, to a one-bedroom apartment in the basement of a brownstone on the Upper West Side. He'd intended to move out months earlier, but then his father had died, and amid all the emotional turmoil surrounding that, Kevin simply hadn't been able to face up to the task of finding a place.

Affixed to the refrigerator door, held neatly in place there by magnets, were the latest crayon-scrawled creations of Genevieve Françoise, Eugènie's four-year-old niece. Eugènie had reached the age of terminal baby lust, no doubt about that. They'd bought the house in Roslyn as a home to raise kids in. Thank god they were getting the divorce before they'd actually had any. What a godawful nightmare that would've been. To be honest about it, Kevin had always harbored mixed feelings about children, feelings Eugènie had always been wont to caustically ascribe to his wanting to be the child of the family himself.

And maybe she was right. "Just look at you!" she'd exclaim. "Just look at all of you in comics. The way you dress—like children. The junk food you gorge yourself on. The way none of you *drink,* for god's sake. And the video games, and the role-playing games, and the unending hours of junk movies and worthless TV."

The house was full of frogs, scores of them, frogs of every conceivable size and description that she'd collected or been given over the years. There were frog magnets on the refrigerator and a frog calendar on the adjoining wall. There was a frog planter and frog bookends in the family room, and a frog-shaped telephone on Eugènie's dressing table upstairs. Whenever anyone spotted a frog anywhere, they invariably bought it and sent it to Eugènie to help assure there'd be no end to the plague. There was something positively weird about it, easily as weird as staying up for days and nights on end playing Wizard Quest or some other role-playing game.

When Kevin was seven, vacationing in the Adirondacks with his folks, he used to catch giant bullfrogs and keep them prisoner in the boathouse in large tin cans. Every day he'd go down there and tie the end of a long reel of nylon fishing line around one of their hind legs, and then slowly, carefully play out the line, letting them swim out with spasmodic kicks across the lake, giving them plenty of time to gorge themselves on flies and insects, giving them the illusion of freedom, before reeling them back in again and shutting them back up in their cans for the night. Come summer's end, of course, he'd let them all go, but today all he had to do was see a frog, or even think of one, to be reminded of what a horrible, sadistic boy he'd been.

Eugènie was sipping tentatively at her coffee-moistened sugar-concoction, waiting impatiently for it to be cool enough to drink. The draft of the property agreement she'd brought home from her attorney's with her, because it seemed "more human," lay inconspicuously folded on the table in front of her. It no doubt stipulated that he would pay for the house while she would own it and live in it. What an uplifting ideology it was, women's lib: in all spheres of life, it enabled them to have it both ways.

There was a shelf full of jars in the breakfast nook, more jars than a person could count, most of them crammed full of the pilfered tidbits that Eugènie liked to bring home from her flights: there were mounds of sugar cubes, of course, with wrappers bearing the United Airlines logo, and then there were the smoked almonds and butter cookies and after-dinner mints, all tastefully sealed inside their aluminum-foil packages. There was a drawerful of matchbooks from every hotel and city she'd ever been. That's how he'd met her, in fact: en route to a fantasy-con in Dallas nearly five years ago. He'd watched her demonstrating the oxygen mask and fallen in love.

Even from the beginning, though, the sex had been terrible. He'd had to eat her practically nonstop for an hour to make her come, and all the while it had been traffic-cop city, do this, do that, a little higher, a little lower, stick your finger in gently while you lick me softly over here. Then she'd claimed that his cock was too big for her, it was so long that it was hurting her ovaries. She had this diabolical way of squeezing her legs against him during fucking to prevent him from moving in and out. She also acquired a mysterious allergy to hair and sweat, thus forcing her to wear a T-shirt whenever they made love. Of course that meant—

"If you want to sign the papers now," suggested Eugènie softly, "I can—"

"No, I don't think so," interjected Kevin. "I think I'd kind of like to read them first."

"It's just what we've already agreed," she replied tolerantly. "But sure, Kev, that's fine."

"You're going to keep the house, right," inquired Kevin, "and I'm going to pay for it?"

"I'm being more than fair, Kev," she answered. "Arthur said, if I wanted, because of you and Octavia, I could—"

"Bang!" exclaimed Kevin dully. "I'm dead! Think you could drive me to the train?"

"What did you think I'd do, Kevin—make you walk?"

CHAPTER 4

▼

A nearly life-size bronze statue of Power Man dominated the reception area, hands placed proudly on massive hips, mighty muscles rippling like strands of steel cable, bronze cape unfurled and flowing majestically in an imaginary wind. When Kevin and his lifelong friend Shelly were at Teaneck High together, and both of them rabid comics fans, they used to ride the bus in after school and spend countless hours here, fidgeting with irrepressible eagerness on these very couches, waiting with excruciating impatience for their favorite freelance writers and artists to pass through the waiting room so that they could hound them unmercifully for free sketches and autographs, waiting for the company's public relations associate to put in an appearance so that she could take them on the official goodwill tour of the premises for the one zillionth time.

While they waited, they would squirm painstakingly over the grimy sketchpads they always carried with them, cluttering the cream-white pages with sketch after ill-proportioned sketch of Power Man and Captain Thunder, straining to capture the nuance of every idealized sinew and bicep, speculating endlessly about upcoming subplots and storylines, and, in the manner of Egyptian whores seeking to ensure their good fortune by surreptitiously inserting coins amid the wrappings of mummies in the Cairo Museum, scrawling their heartfelt wishes for cartooning success on fortune-cookie-sized scraps of paper and planting them amid the billowing folds of Power Man's cape.

More than anything in those youthful bygone days, both Kevin and Shelly had dreamed of working in comic books. Ultimately, through untiring commitment and hard work, Kevin had molded himself into one of Dynamic's top writers, while Shelly had failed to achieve his boyhood ambition and was now managing an H&R Block office in the backwoods of Rego Park.

Now Kevin breezed past the receptionist with a cheery hello and sauntered casually down the gold-carpeted corridor in the direction of Ronald Hinder's office. The corridor's pastel-colored walls were clean and pleasantly corporate, the immaculate surfaces interrupted only occasionally by tastefully matted pen-and-ink drawings of comic-book characters mounted in polished-aluminum frames.

It was all a far cry from what one encountered at the corporate headquarters of Dynamic's chief competitor, Majestic Comics, where every visible surface was so heavily festooned with crudely drawn cartoons and office in-jokes that the entire establishment had the aura of a nursery school for misfits or a hive of delinquent bees. Seven years ago, unfortunately, Majestic had overtaken Dynamic in the marketplace and was now reputed to be outselling Dynamic by two to one. Predictably, there were now dissident voices at Dynamic advocating a slavish copycatting of Majestic's raucous, ragtag style, but Kevin was convinced that the Majestic formula would be the death of comics and that Dynamic had no choice but to hold the line against mediocrity, no matter the short-term costs.

Kevin strolled past the entrance to the production department, pausing in the doorway only long enough to wave hello to one of his favorite paste-up people, then continued down the long hallway and took a right. Octavia's office was located in the same cul-de-sac as Ron's, and Kevin was frankly relieved when he noticed her door was closed. Then he remembered that she was away in France on business for Dynamic—probably doing the trick with Jean-Claude Allande.

Kevin glanced at his watch: it was four-fifteen. Given the time difference, she was probably doing it with Allande this very instant, although with all the coke Allande snorted, god only knew if he could even get it up.

The book on Allande was that he was very eccentric, residing in a drafty Left Bank garret with two strange damsels who had sex with one another a whole lot more frequently than they did with him. Allande slept on one side of the bed, it was said, and did a lot of watching. Notwithstanding all that, he was one hell of an artist, and if it took a *ménage à quatre* with Octavia every few months to keep Allande's creative juices flowing, Kevin was all in favor of her enthusiastically joining in.

Just remembering how good she'd been was enough to make Kevin break out in a sweat. She was the only woman he'd ever known who could bring herself to orgasm just by sucking his cock. And he didn't believe she'd left him for Allande, although the timing sure made it look that way. His feeling was that their relationship had been fine for her so long as he was safely married to Eugènie, but that once he'd begun talking divorce, she'd gotten cold feet. Still, she was an incredible cocksucker and Allande was an absolute genius. So long as Kevin's loss kept Allande happy, it was all right with him.

Hinder's door was also closed, but Kevin could easily tell he was there by the dense gouts of cigar smoke wafting out from beneath the door. In place of ordinary, pedestrian rectangular office-door name plates, Dynamic had opted for clear plastic ones in the shape of thought balloons. On Hinder's door, some free office spirit had taped a really mouth-watering photostat of Dream Lass directly beneath Hinder's name plate, with the result that it now looked as though Dream Lass was absorbed in a sensually wistful reverie of Ron Hinder.

Dream Lass was endowed with huge, pendulous breasts, which was why the guys in production all called her Breast Lass instead. Octavia was easily the hottest fuck in the industry, but that didn't stop her from also being its most ardent upholder of women's lib. When Dream

Lass—a visionary extraterrestrial empath created barely a year ago to provide a much-needed love interest for Power Man—was in her design stage, Octavia had divisively intruded herself into the proceedings by agitating loudly for a costume with less-revealing cleavage and smaller breasts. In the great compromise that ultimately emerged from the ensuing contentious debate—a compromise which Kevin's friendship with the various contending parties greatly helped to facilitate—the actual size of the offending mammaries was reduced only slightly, but an additional button was added to the skintight top of Dream Lass's jumpsuit, greatly reducing the scope of what had been a flagrantly unobstructed V-neck.

Kevin knocked lightly on Hinder's door and let himself in. Like the offices of most editors, it was a small, cluttered, unsightly mess. Everywhere one looked, there were heaps of comic books: Dynamic's, Majestic's, even the output of the horde of tiny independents. An army of Japanese robots massed for war on a bookshelf, and the costly textured corporate wallpaper bristled with buttons bearing such preadolescent slogans as "I am an Extra-Terrestrial" and "Beam me up, Scotty—there are no intelligent life forms down here!" while the wall opposite the bookcase was papered with cover proofs of the comic books Hinder edited, along with a list of the sales figures appropriate to each one.

Like some unkempt latter-day hippie monarch of all he surveyed, Hinder sprawled regally in the heavily upholstered swivel chair behind his desk, the surface of which had long ago vanished beneath a ground cover of disdainfully spurned paperwork, squinting like an owl transfixed by daylight through a pair of rose-tinted heart-shaped eyeglasses, puffing on a humongous Cuban cigar, and looking generally like an unmade bed. The cigars, Kevin knew, had been a gift from Jean-Claude Allande, who'd bought them in London and smuggled them in to Hinder during his last trip to the States.

"Got your message," remarked Kevin evenly. "Problem?"

"We gotta move the Cicada, Kev," proclaimed the Bed lethargically with a tepid sweep of his smoke-filled hand. "It's the Dragon Lady's that time of month. She's hot to get the Cicada on the schedule."

"Creativity takes time. Tell that to the Dragon Lady."

"Bullshit walks, Kev," Hinder shot back. "You know that. Besides, it's not as if you had to *create* the Cicada, for christ's sake. It was part of the package we bought from Champion when they belly-upped. All you—"

"I have to make it work for the Eighties, Ron, remember?" interjected Kevin. "I'm the one who has to find the formula that will make it fly in today's market."

Hinder tenderly extinguished his contraband Havana in an oversized ceramic ashtray that was choked with tar. He whisked off his heart-shaped eyeglasses and scowled at Kevin across his desk. "You've had it for six months now, Kevin. Okay, I know you and Eugènie split, but what the hell is going on?"

"Nothing's going on," exclaimed Kevin. "Nothing. But ever since—"

"Have you done anything at all on the Cicada?" inquired Hinder.

"Oh yeah. Sure," answered Kevin. "I've thought about it a lot. I think I've got a great handle on it. I just need time to—"

"Are you doing anything besides this, Kevin?"

"Besides this?"

"Working the other side of the street, or something like that?"

"No, nothing—just this."

"Kevin, have you written anything at all in the last six months?"

"No. Just the Cicada."

"You broke?"

"No. I'm fine."

"You sure?"

"I'm fine."

"I'd lend you some money, Kev. You don't have to genuflect for the Dragon Lady, you know that."

"You're good people, Ron," replied Kevin softly, nervously brushing a wayward lock of prematurely gray hair away from his eye. "I appreciate that. But no, I'm fine for now. Thanks."

"Can you estimate me a date on the Cicada?"

"Don't force me, Ron. Please. I want the Cicada to be as good as I can make it. I want the Cicada to be Dynamic's next really hot book."

"Perfection's bullshit, Kev. It just gets in the way."

"I know that. You don't—"

"Just work me up an outline, Kevin. Please. Just two or three pages telling me what you're planning—something I can throw into the Dragon Lady's maw. Something she has to digest before she starts bellowing for the first plot."

"You'll have them both," replied Kevin. "Don't worry. I promise."

Hinder retrieved his cigar from the ashtray and began to relight it. Smoke billowed upward, wreathing the robotic sons of Nippon in thick clouds of smoke. "Kevin, just one more thing."

"Yes?"

"You know how this business is. You're up, you're down. You're in, you're out. There are always all kinds of vicious rumors flying around about everybody."

"About me?"

"No, I'm sorry. That's not really what I meant. It was careless of me to phrase it that way and I'm sorry. What I meant is, these aren't the Sixties anymore, Kevin. Comics aren't the way they were when we grew up. The audience is older. The stories are meaner. The good guys aren't so squeaky clean."

"So?"

"So everything I've ever read of yours, Kevin, except maybe the Shambler, but even the Shambler to some extent, although with the Shambler you certainly avoided the worst excesses of that, but with almost everything I've ever read of yours, you're writing about these characters as though they were your closest friends. As if you want to be nice to them, as if you don't want to hurt them. They're just characters, Kevin. Just words on paper. You've got to have what it takes to torture them. You've got to be willing to make them bleed."

CHAPTER 5

▼

It didn't matter how hard he tried, he just couldn't do it. He'd been at it for hours without even making a dent. He made coffee, drank it. He paced the floor talking aloud to himself till his legs hurt. Nothing. Maybe if he just bought a word processor instead of sticking with his damned old Olympia.

The Silver Cicada was one of a score of second-banana characters from the Forties and Fifties that Dynamic Comics had acquired from Champion Comics when Champion went defunct. Kevin's task was to revamp the Cicada to make it contemporary without sacrificing that ineffable yet vital essence that had made it unique and distinctive in its day. Once he'd accomplished that, he would be able to contemplate writing the first new scripts.

As originally conceived in the early 1950s, the Silver Cicada was Rick Norwood, a high-school science teacher who had received his colorful regalia and superscientific crimefighting apparatus from a race of highly evolved cicadalike insects inhabiting an invisible subatomic world. Having adopted the secret identity of the Silver Cicada, Norwood flew through the air on atom-powered wings and battled crime with his flashing fists and distinctive "stinger raygun," until declining sales brought an end to his adventures after about five years.

All of this, Kevin knew, would have to be drastically updated—a psionically powered anti-grav flight module, for example, in place of the wings; pheromonic energy bursts from his fingertips to replace that preposterous raygun; and, without question, a brand-new civilian identity, say a cyberneticist—but no matter how long and how hard he sweated and strained at it, he somehow still couldn't come up with that elusive combination of qualities that would make it all work.

In 1936, George Pfister's Power Man had been the first superhero, a fiery comet ablaze in a bland and lackluster comic book firmament, but now the four-color skies were teeming with superheroes, jostling one another constantly trying to crowd each other out. If you expected to introduce a new one these days, even one like the Cicada whose admittedly marginal place in comic book history could at least assure it some initial reader interest, you had damn well better see to it that it had a special charismatic something its competitors lacked. Above all, you had to make it an extension of yourself somehow, an artistic expression of your own inner being. You had to plumb the depths of who you were and then imbue your character with your own life-essence and make him breathe with you. It was precisely what Kevin had done to perfection with the Shambler just ten years ago.

Admittedly, the Shambler had only survived for thirty-four issues, owing to the fact that its original artist had quit the strip after eighteen months following a series of tiffs over plotlines, leaving Kevin to cope with one hopeless mediocrity after another. Nonetheless, the series had achieved an extraordinary critical success and still remained the accomplishment for which Kevin was best known. Only recently, Dynamic had begun reprinting the thirty-four issues in a series of trade paperbacks, and a Shambler movie was in the works. Kevin's income from the movie would not be spectacular, but the generous creator's bonus that Dynamic had paid him at the completion of negotiations had been especially welcome during these past eight months, when his damned writer's block had prevented him from accomplishing anything else.

The Shambler was a Himalayan snow monster—half-insane yet intensely empathic, nearly blind, lacking even rudimentary organs of speech—who grubbed for gnarled roots and scavenged for vermin amid the trackless, blizzard-swept wastes. His hulking body, swathed in animal pelts, was formed entirely of snow and ice mixed with clots of scraggly vegetation and clumps of earth. A pair of uncomprehending red eyes glowed dully in his head. Only one creature in the entire universe truly loved him: the sensuously beautiful Golden Starling, telepathic birdwoman princess of a time-lost extradimensional realm.

But the Shambler had not always been a monster. Once, he had been Anselm Parnell, a legendary mountain climber and Nobel Prize-winning microbiologist who had been dispatched to the Himalayas by the CIA in hopes of thwarting a sinister scheme by the nefarious Scorpion Brotherhood to fuse Himalayan shamanistic magic with modern microbiological science in the development of a diabolical "entropic life formula" for the creation of a horde of unconquerable abominable snowmen to ravage and overrun the earth.

Perilously making his way to the villains' hidden eyrie of evil amid the looming ice-capped crags above Ladakh, Parnell succeeded in carrying out his mission—but only at the cost of his human life—when an accidental explosion tore apart the evildoers' sanctum, annihilating the Scorpion Brotherhood but also burying the valiant microbiologist beneath tons of avalanching snow and ice.

As he lay there lifeless and unmoving beneath the ice-bound wastes, surrounded by towering pinnacles silently resonating with the eldritch arcane forces built up within them over the course of eons by the Himalayan shamans' mystic chants, the organs and tissues of Parnell's body were slowly permeated, dissolved, replaced by new organs mysteriously generated by the huge stockpile of entropic life formula loosed from its tightly sealed drums by the blast. When, hours—or was it perhaps days?—later, Anselm Parnell finally clawed his way free of his icy tomb, he was no longer human, no longer a living, breathing being of flesh and blood. He was a man, of sorts—but a man forged of weirdling spells, and chemicals, and ice and snow. He could sense … some things. He understood … a little. Occasionally, he had fleeting recollections of the precious humanity he had had—and lost. He could see, but only dimly … could feel others' emotions intensely … but not his own. Lichens hung from him like spiders. His face and chest were smeared with clotted blood. People, when they chanced to see him, fled from him in abject terror—or showered him with flaming firebrands, hoping to melt him or burn him alive.

Until he met the Golden Starling, in issue number eighteen, he was totally, completely alone. When he walked, he shambled, a hideous mockery of the man he had once been. Kevin had been on the verge of christening him the Abomination, but then, in a flash of insight, had made his creation at once more sympathetic, and pathetic, by naming him the Shambling Man—and then simply the Shambler—instead.

Kevin walked into the bathroom and urinated—pissing away all that instant coffee he'd been consuming in the interminable struggle to stay awake—then washed his hands in the sink and splashed cold water in his face. The squirrel scars of his childhood peered cruelly out at him from between the clusters of pus specks that flecked the mirror above the sink.

What had happened to him? Why couldn't he write anymore? Why?

CHAPTER 6

▼

"You don't remember me, do you?"

"Hey, sure I remember. Last time you were here, you shot off a tremendous—"

"No. I didn't. I just wanted to talk."

"Talk?"

"Which is what I want to do now."

"Sure. Fine. But most guys like to show it to me first. I'll bet—"

"I can understand your not remembering me. Really. But I still—"

"Hey, what bullshit? I remembered."

"You didn't …"

"Hey, look. I—"

"… but it's okay."

"I see a whole lot of guys in here, okay? Even though a lot of times I wish—"

"I know. You've got a rough—"

"Ha! You don't know the half—"

"I'm Kevin. Remember? I write comic—"

"Hey! The comic book man! Wow! I—"

The black screen descended, cutting her off from him. Mumbling "fuck" under his breath, Kevin fumbled for a second token and rammed it authoritatively into the coin slot. It thunked home before the screen even reached bottom. The screen whirred in place an instant, then silently rose.

"C'mon, Kevin. Why not ask me to show you my tits?"

"I can't work."

"Huh?"

"I can't work. I haven't been able to write a line for nearly eight months."

"You mean the comics?"

"Right."

"How come?"

"I don't know. I just can't. And when I try—"

"Yeah?"

"—I get so tired I just want to sleep."

"And?"

"So I drink coffee. Lots of it. And then—"

"Kevin?"

"What?"

"You turn me on, you know what I mean? You get my pussy red hot. You don't want to jerk off for yourself, okay. But at least—"

"What's your name?"

"Why?"

"I forgot to ask the last time. This time I wanted to make sure I didn't forget to ask you your name."

"It's Vicki."

"Vicky?"

"Uh-huh."

"It's a nice name. In the third grade I had—"

Once again, the opaque guillotine had begun its descent. Kevin slugged home another token, this time reversing its direction before it was even halfway down.

"Is Vicky your real name?"

"Sure, whattaya think? But—"

"But?"

"But what difference does it make, you know what I mean?"

"Sure, I guess so."

"I don't give a shit if your name's Kevin."

"Okay. But, look, this means a lot to me. I drink the coffee to stay awake. Tons of it. And it works. I do stay awake. But then—"

"Kevin?"

"—then the anxiety hits me. Huge waves of it. It's as though I was going to be destroyed, annihilated. As though some—but I don't let it beat me. I stick with it. I mean in the early months I did let it beat me, but then I got to the point where if I stuck with it, I could handle it. But then even if I do that, the ideas won't come! No matter what I do, no matter how hard I—"

"I thought you said you were a comic book writer."

"I am."

"But how can you be writing anything if you're so—I don't mean to hurt your feelings, Kevin, but it all sounds awfully fucked up."

"But it wasn't always this way, Vicky. It wasn't. I used to write a script a week, for christ's sake. For a living. God damn it, this is my living. It's the only—"

"Then how long have you—"

"Seven and a half months."

She laughed. "You got it figured to the day it started, right?"

"No, not exactly. But I remember the first time it happened to me was on the Psionic Dreadnoughts job. It was the first job I got right—"

The opaque screen glided down again, this time before Kevin even fully realized it, and the lights in the ceiling of his booth blinked on. Kevin had bought and spent three tokens, and although a large part of him yearned to buy more, another large part of him needed time to think. He didn't know how she'd done it, but she'd put her finger right on it: the first job he hadn't been able to do, the first job he'd had to turn back because of his writer's block, was the Psionic Dreadnoughts job they'd assigned him right after his father died.

Kevin unlatched the booth door and stepped outside—into the windowless, teeming sleaze emporium. All around the garishly lighted circumference of a crowded rotunda, girls who looked for all the world like whores, but weren't, posed and strutted suggestively before the entrances to their twin booths, a few of them voluble and gregarious and sassy, but most of them frowsy and wilted after ten or more grueling hours of nonstop work.

As for the patrons—a motley brew of blue-collar workers of all races, servicemen, and grinning office workers with nervous ticks who carried attaché cases and folded newspapers and wore three-piece suits—they milled nervously about under the intimidating scrutiny of "security personnel"—thugs—recruited from the nearby slums, sizing up the girls and purchasing supplies of tokens from the various house cashiers—more thugs—who dispensed them from lofty stools fronted by high counters, like judges doling out dollops of ragged justice in night court.

As each client arrived at his selection and shuffled uncomfortably into his chosen booth, the girl would mash out her cigarette and duck through a curtained entranceway into her booth, adjoining, and a red light would blink on atop the patron's booth to indicate it was in use. Outside in the rotunda, meantime, maintenance workers with sponge mops and scrub buckets roved about in a kind of narcoleptic torpor, making the rounds of the unoccupied booths to sponge the freshly ejaculated semen off the floors and walls.

The Pornomart was an endless fun-house maze of labyrinthine passageways and cul-de-sacs, so similar to one another in appearance that, once having found one's way in, it was by no means that simple to find one's way out. Everywhere the eye fell, tawdry hand-painted signs ennobled with black-and-gold glitter—and illuminated by multicolored lightbulbs flashing on and off in sequence to create the kinetic illusion of an ever-revolving halo of light—proclaimed the twenty-five-cent token price of long ago, despite the fact that the actual price of the house entertainments was two dollars per minute and the only thing a quarter would buy you now was thirty seconds of viewing time on a pay-as-you-watch porno TV.

Kevin descended a staircase lined with giant poster-size photos of the reigning sex stars and found himself on a small mezzanine over-looking the Pornomart's smut shop, with its awesome array of maga-zines, dildos, and porn tapes, catalogued according to fetish and designed to satisfy every conceivable taste. Retracing his steps back to the staircase, Kevin passed by an empty room where a projection TV flickered with grainy footage of a nubile white teenager fellating a gnarled and warted old black man easily five times her age, and then cast a hasty glance through a half-open dressing-room door, where a G-stringed performer with sequined eyelids was studiously preparing herself for the continuous live all-night sex show upstairs.

As Kevin finally arrived at the lobby floor—elbowing his way through a crush of terminally horny college boys clustered raucously around a visiting porn queen for the chance to pose with her for Polaroids for fifteen dollars a shot—he could hear the Pornomart's cacophonous loudspeakers announcing the Manhattan debut of Amanda and her python about to unfold on the live sex stage up on the fourth floor.

CHAPTER 7

▼

Propelled by their ultrasonic boot jets, the Thunder Hounds swooped and soared across the TV screen, while Inferno, the malevolent Death Dragon of the Evil Empire, roared after them. God, the production qualities of today's animation were terrible, but Kevin had to admit the Thunder Hounds were still pretty neat.

His living-room floor was strewn with videocassettes—everything from triple-X-rated movies to crime shows, sitcoms to soap operas, talk shows to Saturday-morning cartoons. Old *Shadow* radio tapes that he regularly acquired by mail order were piling up faster than he could possibly play them, and the stacked-up cartons of complimentary comic books from Dynamic and Majestic Comics were seriously threatening to crowd him out of house and home.

Except for the flickering cool fire of the TV set, the living room was dark. Indeed, located as it was in the basement apartment of a West Side brownstone, it was nearly always dark, and a trifle dismal, but after breaking up with Eugènie, Kevin knew that he'd been fortunate to latch onto an affordable sublet only a block from the park.

Kevin zapped off his VCR and sat alone in the darkness. A junky old advertising clock for Cat's Paw heels and soles from the 1950s, an artifact from his bachelor days, eyed him wanly from the wall of the adjoining kitchen. Eugènie had loathed that clock, and yet she was gone now, while it still kept time perfectly after all these years.

Kevin rose from the couch and switched on the dilapidated old pole lamp which provided the living room with its only real light. The hardware that bolted the individual lamps to the pole from the inside no longer gripped properly, so that the four hundred-watt bulbs, their diverse angles now uncontrollable, shone off in all directions, slicing the room into discomfiting swatches of light. From the center of the living room's lone bare-brick wall, definitely the most charming feature of the entire apartment, an ocher-and-red spirit mask from New Guinea gazed down with an enigmatic but generally benevolent expression, safeguarding the apartment and all its occupants against maleficent spirits, or at least that's what its anthropologist owner had claimed when he hastily sublet Kevin the apartment so that he could return to complete his doctoral fieldwork among a once-cannibalistic Fly River tribe.

Kevin wondered if the guardian spirit's powers extended to exerting any protective control over heart attacks. Maybe if his father had only had this spirit mask watching over him, he wouldn't have had his heart attack. Or maybe if he *had* had it, at least it wouldn't have killed him.

Even when Kevin was a youngster, his father had known that one day he was going to die of a heart attack. The wonder of it, they all said afterward, was that he had managed to live for as long as he did. As far back as Kevin could remember, he and his mother and sister would tiptoe around him, cushioning him against the shocks of life, insulating him from bad news, scrupulously watching his diet, not making demands, terrified that at any moment one of them might do something that would take him from them. For hours at a time he would sit, alone and unapproachable, among his rare leather-bound books and crystal silver-topped inkwells, listening to Brahms and Beethoven, reading the newspaper, studying the latest addenda to the tax code, conferring on the phone with clients, writing reports sometimes late into the night.

Yet, notwithstanding all that, he was also a warm, loving, gregarious man who took Kevin fishing in the Adirondacks countless times when he was little, before his sister was born, despite the undeniable fact that Kevin's mother became a nervous wreck whenever he and his father went out in a boat. And except on those nights when he was away on business, nothing could deprive him of the opportunity of reading Kevin a bedtime story before he went to bed.

Kevin stretched out full-length on the living-room couch and tried to recapture some of the details of the earliest stories they'd read. It was all but impossible to remember anything that had happened so long ago, but Kevin still harbored definite, if somewhat dim, recollections of a penguin, or was it a pelican, and an outlandish exclamatory phrase that went "'Wowie kaplowie!' said Flibberty Gibbet." And Kevin also remembered being read the exploits of a plucky barnyard rooster named Antonio, and his mother had reminded him only recently that he'd cried his eyes out at the story of a tiny baby owl that got lost in the woods. When Kevin grew too old for children's stories, he and his father began reading the classics together: *Moby-Dick,* and *The Last of the Mohicans,* and *Huckleberry Finn.* Kevin's gift from his father when he graduated from elementary school and entered junior high had been a leather-bound set of the Encyclopaedia Britannica's *Great Books.*

Years later, after Kevin had dropped out of college and begun writing comic books, he'd always thought of them as loving gifts for his father, as if each small story he wrote were a pebble piled up against some insurmountable debt.

Lying there in the cluttered brownstone apartment—with the spirit mask and the Cat's Paw clock and the four wayward lights of the pole lamp like an eerie quartet of light sabers coldly dismembering the room—Kevin realized, with startling clarity, that, at bottom, his stories had all been crafted for an audience of one. No wonder he had been afflicted with writer's block since his father's death! With his father gone, there'd simply been no one left to write for!

CHAPTER 8

▼

When Kevin awoke, there was a smattering of rain on his window, and the crimson digits of his clock radio glowed 1:30 PM. Kevin had been up all night until five, by turns agonizing over the Silver Cicada, getting nowhere, and taking hour-long breaks watching TV. There was always the tendency, especially when the writing was not going well, to extend the hours of sleeping and wakefulness later and later, so that almost before one knew it, one had turned night into day. During one particularly frustrating period in his mid-twenties lasting nearly two years, Kevin's sleep cycle had actually degenerated into one of going to sleep at 7:30 in the morning and rolling out of bed around 4:00 PM. Kevin vividly recalled groping his way sleepily to the telephone to contact his various editors before they left work for the day, then showering and dressing around six in the evening and eating breakfast while watching the evening news on TV. Once you'd dug yourself a hole like that, it was hard to climb out of it—by setting the alarm clock and forcing yourself to get up a few hours earlier, for example—because writing required intense concentration, and Kevin simply could not concentrate unless he'd had a full eight hours' sleep. Kevin referred to his night-into-day cycle as his "submarine mode," because it came to seem so isolating and oppressive, like living alone in a submarine at the bottom of the sea.

In the wake of his father's death, Kevin had become a begrudging devotee of an all-night home shopping channel on cable TV. Who in god's name stayed up to shop at those hours, Kevin couldn't even begin to guess, and yet, more often than not, he'd phone in and buy something, anything to distract himself from his frustration and solitude. By the time the purchases were actually delivered, four to six weeks later, Kevin had usually forgotten what it was he'd bought, and that made it even more fun, like receiving a surprise gift from an unknown admirer every three or four days. As for the purchases themselves—the midget electric trains and the mink Teddy bears, the lush baskets of silk flowers and the collectible dolls—all of which Kevin rationalized as future holiday gifts for the secretaries at Dynamic Comics or for the women who might one day enter his life, they added a special class of clutter to a living space already piled high with clutter, like poignant offerings for a kitsch afterlife in a pop-culture tomb.

Sometime during those ungodly twilight hours preceding the crack of noon, Ron Hinder had left a message on Kevin's answering machine, but Kevin knew there was little point in trying to return the call until 4:00 PM, which was the time Hinder usually returned from lunch. It must be rough, mused Kevin, to have a job that required you to eat lunch three or four times a day. Of course, the editors invariably also managed, through their control of their company's freelance work assignments, to steal the choicest assignments for themselves to supplement their incomes—and to cajole the most popular artists into collaborating with them—the clear but unspoken inference being that artists who cooperated in this manner would never lack work. And since many of the editors all but doubled their incomes in this manner, the comics companies made no real effort to curb the practice since it enabled them to keep editorial salaries low. Typically, the editors were failed writers who would probably starve to death if they ever had to give up their day jobs and depend for their livelihoods on freelance work. Hinder, in particular, was a strictly bush-league talent, but he still made more money writing comics than Kevin did.

Along around three, however, Kevin tried Hinder's number, and lo and behold, the star was in.

"Listen, Kevin," exclaimed Ron, "I've got something here. Could be you could do us both a favor."

"What?"

"We just came out of an editorial meeting. We had a few late shippers last month, so the Dragon Lady wants fill-ins on every book in the house. I was hoping you could maybe do a Mega-Man for me. I know years ago you wrote half a—"

"What about the Cicada?" asked Kevin. "I thought there was all this heat on—"

"Look, Kevin, there is. I'm not saying throw the Cicada in the trash-can. But maybe it's making you crazy having to focus on it day after day. Maybe it would help you to let it percolate for a week. Plus I need this fill-in, Kevin, and I know you could do a bang-up job on it. And besides"—Ron's voice lowered—"I'm assuming you could use the damn paycheck, Kevin. Jesus Christ, buddy, besides some development money on the Cicada, have you pulled a paycheck out of here in the last six months? I—"

"Twenty-two pages?"

"Twenty-four. It's new format."

"Can I do something offbeat?"

"Sure, why not? I mean, I don't think I want to see twenty-four pages of Mega-Man feedings the pigeons in Central—"

"I wouldn't do that and you know it."

"Look, Kevin, just run the character through his paces for me, that's all. He's got a new power. I'll messenger you out the last four or five issues so you can get a good look at it. And don't use Celeste Diamond—you know, his girlfriend?—because Patrick's planning on having her suffer brain damage when he takes his goggles off and probably die in a flaming oxygen tent three months later, in time for the Annual."

"Can I use the Shambler?"

"The Shambler? In an issue with Mega-Man?"

"Why not?"

"Because it's mixing genres, Kevin. Mega-Man's straight superhero, the Shambler's horror, or fantasy, whatever. More often—"

"But if I think it works?"

"You have an idea?"

"No. It's—"

"Oh, what the hell, Kevin. Sure, why not? Don't even call me with a springboard. Just try to have some fun with it. Surprise me. Leave off the Cicada for a week or so. Just run some riffs with Mega-Man and earn yourself a few bucks."

"Thanks, Ron. I appreciate it."

"Don't be ridiculous. You're a pro. It's just—"

"Except that I haven't—been producing lately. I'm sorry. I owe you."

"Forget it. You want me to voucher it for you so your check will be waiting when you hand in the job?"

"Please. That—"

"Done. Listen, forgive me. People are pouring in here. Melinda is attaching electrodes to my genitals. She—"

Kevin could hear the titter of secretarial mirth in the background. He flashed on Melinda's purple lipstick and lone gold tooth.

"I've got three books I've got to turn in to production by five o'clock or they won't ship. And one of them's *Apocalypse*. I don't think I can make it."

"You'd damn sure *better* make it," trilled Melinda in the background.

"You all set, then, Kevin?" asked Hinder.

"All set," replied Kevin. "Take it easy."

And they hung up.

For the rest of the day, Kevin focused his entire concentration on Mega-Man, but no matter how much he concentrated, he never seemed to get beyond square one. Mega-Man was one of a slew of dependable old-line superheroes who'd recently been made over by company edict into grim vigilantes in order to capitalize on a mushrooming trend in sales. Gone, in all likelihood forever, were the perfect, morally inspiring heroes of Kevin's youth, with their unbreakable codes against killing, their willingness even to temporarily break off a battle with an extraterrestrial super-conqueror, if need be, in order to rescue innocent bystanders from flying glass. In today's cheapened moral comics climate, by contrast, the so-called hero battered his enemy senseless in Grand Central Station and then stood on the platform ruminating over whether to rescue his vanquished adversary from beneath the wheels of an oncoming train.

The horrifying thing was, it all sold like a house afire—so much so that, of all Dynamic's main characters, only Power Man had been kept aloof from the trend, and that was chiefly owing to his revered flagship status and the immense licensing revenues derived from his use in kiddie cartoons and children's toys. When it came to comic book sales, however, Power Man was definitely yesterday's news.

Today, there was scarcely a hero on the racks a boy could look up to, hardly a character on sale a man could be proud to call "father" or "friend." Alone among the ranks of the murderous, enraged vigilantes, only the heroes Kevin wrote about were still wholesome, honorable people whose lives, both as private citizens and as crimefighters, were beyond reproach. They might exclaim "Great Scott!" in a moment of stress, but they didn't use swear words or flout the law. They were never tempted to deviate from their high moral code. They could never marry, of course, because that would inevitably lead to villainous reprisals against those they loved, but insofar as they had relationships with women, they were warm and respectful. And to the extent that their lives had been made entangled and miserable by previous writers, Kevin did his level best to even out their problems and put them on a tranquil, even keel again.

For as long as Kevin could remember, he had always conversed aloud with himself, sometimes in lengthy, drawn-out "discussions," with Kevin alternately espousing at least two points of view. Whenever he plotted a new story, Kevin would pace the floor relentlessly, vociferously scrutinizing the fledgling creation from every angle, straying off on long tangents, acting out all the parts.

A story could have its beginnings anywhere: a childhood memory, an imagined line of dialogue, the sight of a homeless old woman asleep in the street. It was conjuring that first precious piece of the puzzle, making that divine leap from nothing to something, that was the hardest part. After that, additional pieces of the puzzle came more easily; once one had fitted together half a dozen pieces, the rest was all downhill.

But getting that first piece required excruciating concentration, concentration that was hard enough to attain if you loved the main character, let alone if you disliked him or if, every time you tried to concentrate, you kept being distracted by something else.

Anxiety and upset were death to a writer, and yet to Kevin it seemed that these days he was nearly always upset. Every time he tried to focus on Mega-Man, he'd find himself thinking about Eugènie and their pending divorce. Sometimes he'd pace back and forth across his living room for over an hour—eleven paces one way, eleven back—before finally awakening to the fact that he was no longer working on the story and making a concerted effort to get back on track. Then worrisome thoughts about money would intervene. Kevin would start worrying about money, adding up his projected income and subtracting his anticipated expenses through the end of the year. Over the years, Kevin had come to realize that money often served as a soothing stand-in for other kinds of worries, worries that tended to evoke an infinitely more disturbing anxiety as the result of being far less tangible and consequently far less amenable to some reassuring semblance of rational control.

All at once, Kevin was aware of being extremely tired. That's what invariably happened when he paced for too long: he'd become exhausted and have to lie down awhile and take a nap. By the time he awoke, it might well be dinnertime, time to sit down in front of the TV set and eat a Weight Watchers frozen dinner over a bed of rice, a meal he always enjoyed even though he was fairly skinny and had no need to lose weight.

In this manner, entire days could pass, even weeks, without his having written a solitary word.

Kevin strolled out to the mailboxes and pored through the afternoon's mail. In addition to a printed circular from his congressman detailing all the things he had done in recent months to keep America great, there were two other items: a renewal notice from a weekly comics-industry trade paper, *The Comics Gazette,* and a heart-rending appeal from Captain Jacques-Yves Cousteau for funds to assist him in making desperately needed repairs to his ship. Kevin filed the congressman and Cousteau missives in the nearest trashcan. He had no interest whatever in politics and, while he did have a healthy respect for Captain Cousteau, and had once even responded to a heartfelt plea from the good Captain for a twenty-dollar contribution to help clean up the world's seas, he had since been the recipient of so many urgent appeals for additional funds with which to refit, refurbish, or repair the *Calypso,* that he had begun to harbor serious doubts whether the Captain's venerable old ship was seaworthy at all. As for the day's remaining piece of mail, the renewal notice, Kevin resolved to take that issue under advisement. He approved, generally speaking, of the way the *Gazette* covered industry news, but he had been altogether displeased with a recent series of articles they'd published praising the very trends he abhorred for helping to attract older readers to comics and thereby enhancing their prospects of escaping the confines of the specialized comic book shops and being granted permanent shelf space in the nation's conventional bookstores.

Kevin was getting nowhere with Mega-Man and he knew it, and that awareness sent widening ripples of anxiety coursing through him. Writing was not like chopping firewood or engaging in any other workaday task. In writing something, especially in the very earliest phases of it, a writer was completely at the mercy of his imagination, in the grip of mental and psychological processes over which he exercised no control and only barely understood, whereas in the case of chopping firewood, or addressing envelopes, or even carrying out a task requiring extraordinary manual skill, one could rest secure in the knowledge that completing the task was only a matter of time.

Not so with writing, at least not the creative kind. With that kind of writing, although admittedly the polishing phases required mere craftsmanship and the tiresome typing and retyping of the various drafts was no more than clerical drudgery, the initial spark that gave life to the process was a thing of wonder that no human being on earth had the power to control. All one could do was concentrate, and pray that it came, like a gift.

Kevin struggled to wipe his mind clear of everything but the story, strained to envision into existence that one lone infinitesimal atom of inspiration that he could mold and expand into an imaginative creation of the required length, even as the anxious wellspring within him swelled into a rising and panicky tide.

And then suddenly, the idea hit him: he recalled a Captain Ironfist story he'd read six or seven years ago in which, in the course of a tavern brawl, the hero made the acquaintance of a brave young warrior who was returning to Vale Sinister, the land of his birth, determined to slay a loathsome monster that dwelled there. Arriving together, ultimately, at the monster's lair, the two adventurers finally slew the beast after a furious battle, rescuing, in the process, a beautiful woman who appeared to have been enslaved by it. Far from being grateful, however, the maiden was horrified: as she became hideously transformed into a withered hag, and then a heap of bones, before their very eyes, she managed to explain that the slain monster had been a benevolent creature, not an evil one, and that it was only the mutual love they had borne one another that had enabled her to maintain the illusion of her long-vanished youth. And as she disintegrated forever into a small mound of dust, she gasped out the most horrifying truth of all—that she was herself the warrior's mother, and that the warrior was the slain monster's son. Shattered by these revelations, and aghast at the patricide he had committed, Captain Ironfist's companion wrenched his dagger from its sheath and fatally stabbed himself before Captain Ironfist could stop him.

The old Captain Ironfist story seemed like a made-to-order answer to Kevin's dilemma. All he'd have to do would be to change the locale from the medieval sword-and-sorcery world of Captain Ironfist to an alien dimension or planet, transform the brave young warrior into the intrepid young commander of an interstellar starfighter, and, for the most diabolically ingenious touch of all, substitute his own Shambler for the misunderstood monster. But since it would be unthinkable to even dream of killing off the Shambler, Kevin realized he would have to locate his saga in some sort of alternate "parallel universe" whose inhabitants included doppelgangers of many of the people and creatures of Earth.

Kevin was very excited about his plans for the story. It seemed to him that at last the long drought was over and that the magic he had yearned for had finally come back.

CHAPTER 9

▼

The black panel descended, cutting him off from her. The booth lights blinked on again. Kevin rammed home a token and the lights blinked out again, the panel rose.

"Isn't there any way to keep that thing from—"

"Don't get mad. Sure."

"What?"

"Simple. Just drop in all your tokens at once."

"It'll stay up?"

"Uh-huh."

"I like you, Vicki."

"I like you, too. I just wish you came here more often."

"What's my name?"

"You're the comic book guy. I'm not that good at names."

"Kevin. Now, do I put all my tokens in now, while it's up—"

"Sure, go ahead."

"—or do I wait for—"

"No, now's fine. But you're the boss. Do whatever you like."

Kevin thrust his hand into his pocket, pulled out his remaining five tokens, heard them go chug-chug-chug, chug-chug, as he rammed them impatiently into the slot.

"Five?" she asked.

"Five. Right."

"I wish you had more."

"I guess I do, too, but—"

"We'd have more time."

"It's expensive."

She shrugged.

"I want to tell you about my story."

"What?"

"The story I was starting to tell you about when—"

"You're not a fag or anything, are you, Kevin?"

"Me?"

"Because, I mean, with a name like Kevin—"

"No, of course I'm not a—"

"Don't you want to see my tits, Kevin? Don't you even want to see my pussy? You could jerk—"

"It's my time, right—my money?"

"Hey, okay."

"I get to use it any way I want?"

"Sure."

"I need to tell you about this. I need to tell you about the story. Because—"

"Okay, why?"

"—because it was really you who put me onto it. It was you who got me out of it."

"I what?!"

"Look, I don't expect you to remember. Sometimes I'm a little dense, maybe, but I'm not a dope. I know an awful lot of guys come through here. I—"

"I did what, Kevin?"

"I couldn't work for eight solid months. I was going crazy trying to figure out what was wrong. It should've been obvious. It was right in front of me. But you clued me in to the fact that my writer's block started right after my father—"

"You're a writer, right?"

"You know that. I just said that."

"Comic books, right?"

"God damn it, Vicki—"

"You write the words that go inside those little balloons?"

"I write the script. Like a television script. Except—"

"You mean the cartoons?"

"No. Comic book stories. Like, have you ever heard of—"

"No, I don't think—"

"—the Shambler, or—"

"I don't think so, no."

"It doesn't matter. I'm a writer. I haven't been able to write for months. Almost eight months. At least I *hadn't* been able to, until you put your finger on it for me. I guess I must've told you about my father, because you made me realize that when I started to have trouble writing was right after my father died. So I thought about that a lot. And, damn it, it hit me. It was so obvious. I adored my father. When I was a boy, he used to read to me. Stories. Books. When I started junior high, he bought me a set of the *Great Books*. Aristotle. Shakespeare. Dostoevski. An important part of our life together was his reading me stories. For a lot of kids, you know, their mother reads them stories. But for me, it was my father. So it was very important to me. I can't help thinking that it must've been very important to him. When I grew up, I felt I had this incredible debt to repay. I guess I repaid it, partly, by becoming a writer, a person who wrote stories. And deep down, whenever I wrote a story, I think I must've been really writing for him, for my—"

"He read them?"

"Of course he read them. Whenever I had dinner at my folks' house, I would bring copies over. My mother went crazy over them. She always wanted to read them right away, not even wait for dinner. My dad would set them aside for later. He always promised me he would read them later. So I knew I was always bringing him pleasure, you know what I mean? In some way, I was paying back the love and the pleasure he'd always given to me. Even though I—the Shambler, say— had an audience of hundreds of thousands, he was my real audience, the audience of one I was really, really writing for. Then when he died—"

"That is sad."

"—I guess somewhere, deep down, I felt I just had no reason to write anymore, what was the point, really, now that he was dead? So something inside me clicked off, and I—I just stopped. But once I'd talked to you about it, like gotten it off my chest or something, and you put me in touch with what was really going on, I guess getting in touch with it made it possible for me to deal with it somehow. What- ever had clicked off, all at once it clicked on again. I got a Mega-Man assignment, and—snap—I wrote it like that. As a matter of fact, Dynamic Comics is a ten-minute walk from here. I just handed—"

"You said your father used to read you comic book stories, right?"

"No, books. *King Arthur. Moby-Dick.* He—"

"You didn't say he used to read you comic books?"

"My father? Are you kidding? He thought they were junk. When I was a kid, he would hardly let them into the house, for Pete's sake. My mother—"

"Then who read you the comic books?"

"Nobody read me the comic books, Vicki. They have—"

"I must've got confused. I—"

"That's what I think."

"Huh-!?"

"I don't think you were listening. I was trying to explain I was grate- ful, damn it! To thank you! To explain how much I appreciated that, intentionally or not, you'd—"

Kevin's time was up. Already the opaque black panel had begun its swift descent.

"But instead you—"

In spots where the panel's painted surface had been worn away, tiny flecks of light shone through from the other side, Vicki's side, like the wistful incandescence of time-lost stars.

"I can't understand for the—"

The lights on Kevin's side of the booth blinked on.

CHAPTER 10

▼

"Damn it, Kevin!" Ron Hinder shouted. "I am doing you a *favor!*"

"You could've fooled me," retorted Kevin angrily.

Seated at the long wooden typewriter table in his kitchen, beside his yellow telephone, Kevin could envision Hinder in his mind's eye, sprawled in his office swivel chair like a sated whore in bed, wreathed in a choking miasma of cigar or cigarette smoke, the door of his comics-strewn cubicle locked and barred against the swirling mob of traffic managers, artists, messengers, and production people, all of whose livelihoods were being kept in a continual state of tumultuous disarray and upheaval by his unvarying irresponsibility, lateness, and total disorganization. He was probably still wearing the rose-tinted heart-shaped eyeglasses, although Kevin realized he might also have changed them by now, since Hinder invariably sported some new set of eyewear weirdness about every other week.

"Kevin, are you listening to me?" inquired Ron.

"What?" blurted Kevin.

Somewhere in the background, Kevin made out a loud, muffled thump—no doubt an attempt by some conscientious manager, mindful of Dynamic's production schedules, to break down Hinder's door with a battering ram.

"I can't use the story, Kevin. I just can't."

"I heard that. But why not?"

"Damn it, Kevin! I told you why not! You ripped off Art Glazer's story! This Mega-Man job you handed in is a direct—"

"It isn't, damn it!"

"Look, Kevin, this is such an incestuous business, it's practically inevitable. Everybody cops from somebody else once in a while. And you've been dry for a while, Kevin. I understand that. But you came too close this time, Kev, that's all. The Dragon Lady would have me pilloried if I ran this, for christ's sake. But at least I'd have an out. I could say my writer sold it to me and I didn't know. But you know the fan press, Kev. The *Gazette*. The *Courier*. They'd eat you for breakfast, Kevin. You'd have no—"

"I didn't plagiarize Art Glazer's story, dammit!"

"Look, Kevin, it's me—Ron. I'm on your side. You transposed the visuals, you slotted in your own main characters, you spliced in that almost-love scene, which was nice. I'd like to see more shit like that from you. But beyond that, it's plain as the fucking nose on—"

By now Kevin was very exasperated. It was hard enough to get to talk to Ron Hinder on the phone these days, forget getting a face-to-face appointment with him, but it seemed even when he finally did get to talk with him, all Hinder gave him was a face full of grief. Kevin was trying hard, trying hard to keep his temper from getting out of control. "I recall Glazer's story vaguely," he remarked. "It came out about seven or eight years ago. The—"

"Eighteen months."

"What?"

"It came out eighteen months ago. I'm staring right at it. Everybody and his little brother read it. It was nominated for a damn—"

"What do you want me to do?"

"There's plenty of time. There's no deadline on it. It's just a fill-in. But if you take my advice, you'll—"

"Redo it?"

"Start over. Toss it in the trashcan and go from scratch. You'll be better off, believe me. You hand in a job that evokes one from ten years ago, that's an *hommage*. Nobody's going to give you a hard time. But—"

"Okay," murmured Kevin, "I hear you."

"Should I throw—"

"Whatever you want," replied Kevin. "I'll be in touch."

Kevin hung up the phone and poured himself a cup of instant. His eyes had begun to burn—the way they often did when he got upset—and he was breathing hard. He gulped down the coffee, pausing between gulps only long enough to polish off the remains of a box of chocolate-covered marshmallow cookies. Notwithstanding the infusion of caffeine, the phone conversation and the sugar were beginning to put him to sleep. Kevin was just beginning to contemplate a midday nap when the phone rang again.

"Kevin! How the fuck are you, you pathetic, miserable asshole?"

The voice on the other end of the line was indisputably Jordan Mason's. Indeed, the machine-gun verbal velocity and the razor edge of vituperative camaraderie that went with it could not even conceivably have originated anywhere else. Kevin could picture him easily, all lanky six-feet-seven inches of him, bedecked in costly Native American jewelry and ensconced fetus-like in his globular red-plexiglass womb chair in the den of his extensively remodeled hacienda on the outskirts of Santa Fe. It was a home overflowing with valuable Indian artifacts and eerily populated by life-sized models of Mason's blood-chillingly scarifying creations: the fearsome horde of science-fiction-movie monsters—such as the man-devouring hydra from *Otherworld* and the soul-stealing sand-scorpion from *Star-Lost Marauder*—to which his bizarrely brilliant imagination and sculptural genius had lovingly given birth, and which had made him not only rich, but a Hollywood legend as well.

Jordan was not exactly an easy man to be friends with—indeed, he had tossed more than one of them through his solarium window in moments of pique—but the flip side of his preadolescent vulgarity and unbridled volatility included an ostentatious generosity and a ferocious loyalty that made him a good man to know in a pinch. And despite the penchant for brutally savage maliciousness that had become his hall-mark—exemplified by a near-mythic incident in which he had staged an impromptu "audition" of a lifelike slimy extraterrestrial "sea-boa" for the movie *Destination: Oceanstar* by arranging for it to attack an unsuspecting nubile young starlet while she showered in her mobile dressing room—he nonetheless had numerous friends in the film busi-ness, although admittedly not quite as many friends as enemies. If he ever needed an escape hatch from comic books, Kevin reasoned, Jordan Mason would be an invaluable friend.

"What's going on, Jordan?" exclaimed Kevin brightly—or at least that's what he had begun to exclaim when he was interrupted by that telltale click that told him Mason had cut him off. But only tempo-rarily. Jordan Mason had four incoming lines on his phone, and it seemed he was constantly receiving calls on at least two or three of them. In the case of brand-new acquaintances—or Hollywood moguls—Mason sometimes managed to summon up the uncharacter-istic civility to bark out some slight warning, such as "Be right back!" before switching lines, but with virtually all his other acquaintances he tended to forgo that nicety in favor of just clicking in and out without prior warning, often juggling as many as four ongoing conversations at once.

"What's going on, Jordan?" inquired Kevin, when he heard his line click open.

"Kevin, you rancid old shithead, is that you?"

"Yes. Kevin."

"Oh, jeez, Kev. Right ba—"

Click.

"Kev, what the fuck you want, guy?" snapped Mason when he finally cut back in a minute later.

"You called me," replied Kevin.

"Oh, balls! Jesus! I called you! What the sleazy fuck, Kevin? I had movie monsters on the brain, man, and I flashed on you. What's going down with you, man? You still spraying Lysol on those hotel toilet seats?"

"This hasn't been all that great a week, Jordan."

"Jesus fucking Christ, Kev! I mean it about the toilet seats, man. You can't imagine how many people I've told that to. That fucking gonzo weirdness of yours is a fucking guffaw-getter extraordinaire, man. It is the bona fide life of the party. Whatever you do, don't ever give it up."

"Jor—"

"Seriously, Kevin, you have got to think about cutting that shit out, man. It is totally gonzo maximum weirdness. It—"

"Jordan, look. I'm not—"

"Oh, balls! You're bummed! Is that what the fuck I'm hearing now? You're—"

"Yes."

"What the shit for, Kev? The divorce? C'mon, man. That's nothing. Stop being a fucking wimp. Why, I've had three—"

"You've had five."

Click.

"Five?"

"Five."

"You're sure? You've kept count?"

"That's what you told me. That's what you told the interviewer for—"

"Who?"

"—for *Cinema Masterworks* magazine."

"I did? Five?"

"Five."

"Okay, so I said it. But did I make it up, or—"

Click.

"Kevin, no way should you let the divorce fucking bum you, man. First off, I met her once. She's a wimpy piece of shit. You hear me? A hank of mousy hair and no tits. Nothing. And take it from me, I know French girls, Kevin. If—"

"I can't write anymore, Jordan. I haven't written a story since my father—"

"Your—"

"Eight months. I haven't written a story in eight months. I'm broke. It's making me crazy. I—"

"You haven't written a story in eight months?"

"I wrote one. Last week. It just got bounced."

"Why?"

"I—I don't know."

"You want me to call the asshole editor who bounced it and tell him to go fuck himself?"

"No."

"You getting any pussy, Kevin?"

"What?"

"Creativity requires pussy, Kevin. I thought I'd already taught you that. Creativity has pussy as a fundamental prerequisite, you understand what I'm saying to you? Not too much. Too much makes you weak in the knees. But you gotta have something, Kevin. Something. More than a whiff, but not so much it makes you weak in the knees."

"Jordan, honestly, I don't—"

"Every one of my monsters, Kev? They all originate as cunt. You know what I mean—cunt? Cunt with jaws, Kevin, cunt with teeth, cunt with all kinds of swords and razor blades sticking up out of those slimy lips. It's basic, man. Absolutely basic. But you gotta go after it with integrity, man. Otherwise—"

Click.

"You're there, right?"

"I'm here."

"Good. I want you to come out here, Kevin. I've just remodeled the guest room. Got a whole floor-to-ceiling shelf in there to hold my awards."

"Jordan, listen—"

"No back talk, Kevin. You know how I hate it when you start talking back. You just fly on out here, man. We're gonna fatten you up on cunt, that's all. Fatten you up on cunt and send you back to the Big Asshole to write your ass off."

"Jordan, wait. Does it still—"

Click.

CHAPTER 11

▼

Kevin spotted her practically the minute he got off the plane in Albuquerque, and even though she was bent over a water fountain seventy-five feet away, he knew immediately that it was her.

"Vicki!" he called out. "It's me!" But instead of acknowledging him, she merely completed her drink and continued briskly down the corridor, clad in a Levi's jacket bedecked with rhinestones, fringed white cowgirl boots, and a pair of factory-faded skintight jeans. Her peroxide-blond curls peeked out like a covey of brazen baby birds from beneath her white Stetson hat, adorned with an iridescent blue-and-green peacock-feather band.

"Vicki!" he called out again, and lumbered after her, weighed down by an overstuffed suitcase and by the Olivetti portable he'd dragged along just in case he was prodded by the urge to write.

Rushing headlong but awkwardly down the airport corridor, Kevin wondered what the hell she was doing there. Had she just flown out from New York, as he had? Surely he would have noticed if she'd been on his plane.

Then, abruptly, the cowgirl turned onto an intersecting corridor and vanished from view. Kevin was sure he'd lost her until he spotted the gift shop. Through an impenetrable thicket of stuffed animals and perfume bottles in the plate-glass window, Kevin suddenly spotted the white Stetson hat. Swatches of stone-washed denim and the gracefully fleeting gestures of a nail-polished hand appeared and disappeared like fragments of a chimerical jigsaw puzzle amid the fluorescent-lit gaps separating the mute denizens of the gift-shop menagerie.

Kevin dashed into the shop, overwhelmed with the desire to speak to her but having no idea what he was going to say. There was a massive stuffed panda inside, and it occurred to—

A steely hand grasped his shoulder tightly from both above and behind. "Jesus Fucking H. Christ, Kevin!" stage-whispered a disapproving voice. "Get real, man! You don't want that!"

Kevin whirled. Festooned with turquoise and silver jewelry, his straight shoulder-length blond hair held in place by a brightly colored silken headband, Jordan Mason loomed above Kevin like an Indian Christmas tree. The denim cowgirl, meanwhile, had pulled a flamingo-colored souvenir tank top off the rack and was in the process of paying the cashier. When she put it on, assuming it would ever actually fit her, huge red capitals spelling out LAND OF ENCHANTMENT would ripple tantalizingly across her gigantic breasts. A hardened tarmac of face powder encrusted her face. From up close, she didn't remotely resemble Vicki. Kevin winced after her as she scooped up her purchase and minced out the door.

"Good god, Kevin!" hissed Mason. "Her face—it'd come off on your clothes!"

They exited the terminal and strode across the parking lot, Jordan setting the pace with his seven-league strides, hands unencumbered and swinging casually at his sides, and Kevin a dozen yards or so behind him, lugging both suitcase and typewriter and straining to catch up. Night-Fang, Mason's purebred Borzoi—named after the Oscar-winning werewolf he'd created for *The Night of the Wolf*— greeted them with a chorus of joyous barks from Mason's jeep.

Among the numerous legends surrounding Mason was that he had once made his living smuggling rare birds across the border from Mexico by drugging them with knockout drops and tucking them away behind a false interior door panel of his car. During one such foray, the story went, he'd successfully eluded U.S. Customs agents after a one-hundred-thirty-mile-an-hour chase, only to suffer a spinout on a rain-slicked road that put him in the hospital for four and a half months and very nearly cost him his life. Nowadays, of course, Mason was an ecology nut and a fierce champion of animal rights, but neither his brush with death nor the passage of time had in any way altered the way in which he liked to drive. New Mexico was made for Mason because the horizon was infinite and there was nothing much around for him to hit.

"I'm sorry the plane was late," shouted Kevin, as they surged across the landscape at rocket speed.

"What?" yelled Mason.

"The plane. I'm sorry it was late. I hope—"

"Forget it," shot back Mason. "Don't even think about it. I practiced on some gash in the lounge, had a high old time."

It was nearly six o'clock, the air was brisk, and the lofty red-sandstone buttes gleamed like minarets in the gathering dusk. New Mexico was a place where everything man had wrought seemed like an eyesore, where the convenience stores and trailer camps seemed like the thoughtless strewings of giants, where every ragged length of fence was an appendicitis scar. The adobe houses so beloved by tourists flecked the landscape like little heaps of shit.

"Hey, Kevin. You know you never told me how you got that shit on your face?"

"Huh—?" winced Kevin.

"Your face. Your nose. They look like they were chewed on by a—"

The jeep jounced wildly long the unpaved road.

"A squirrel," answered Kevin. "When I was still an infant, my mom wheeled me in a baby carriage to Central Park. It was wintertime, snow on the ground, I was in my carriage and she was sitting close by me on a bench. And then suddenly one of those long-rat-tailed squirrels jumped off a tree branch into my carriage and attacked my face."

Jordan Mason sniggered.

"I know it must sound pretty funny, but squirrels are really, you know, rodents. Like rats! I mean, I still like them and everything, but in the wintertime they can get really ravenous. A Parks Department guy told my—"

"So what finally happened, Kevin?"

"My mom grabbed it and flung it away, but not before it took some bites out of my nose and ear. I had plastic surgery. Mostly, people don't—"

"Don't what?"

"Don't notice."

"That's bullshit, Kevin."

"What?"

"They're just being polite."

The sumptuous hacienda that Jordan Mason's monsters had built surmounted a rocky hillside, amid spare clusters of sabino and cotton-wood trees, at the end of a four-mile-long serpentine incline fifty miles northeast of Santa Fe. A patchwork quilt of solar collectors covered the roof, and a louvered sun porch, newly added, sheltered a microcosmic rainforest of exotic plants. Inside, the sprawling rooms with their hand-hewn roofbeams were dominated by full-sized working models of Jordan's monsters, together with framed original sketches, studies, and posters from the films in which they'd appeared. Floor-to-ceiling book-shelves were crammed with portfolios of drawings, film scripts, and, tucked away inside special acid-free storage boxes, the most extensive collection of rare 1930s pulp magazines Kevin had ever seen.

In the gigantic living room, where old hand-crafted Spanish furnish-ings coexisted alongside ones of polished aluminum and plexiglass, dis-play cases and end tables showcased collections of rare Washoe basketry, San Ildefonso pottery, and Hopi Katcina dolls. And just opposite the bizarre couch, which consisted of a colossal ape hand used in the filming of a recent, execrable remake of *King Kong,* an entire long wall was taken up by a state-of-the-art entertainment system including audio- and videotape consoles, a CD-player, and a projection TV. An adjoining room, once a private family chapel, housed a neon-lit jukebox crammed full of Fifties rock 'n' roll hits.

With his irrepressible Borzoi bounding alongside him, Jordan led Kevin up a flight of stairs to the same guest room he'd stayed in just over three years ago, the only other time he'd been here. Mason had kept him up all night that time, berating him for what a fool he was for marrying Eugènie. Setting his bag and typewriter down just inside the doorway, Kevin mused to himself that he'd probably be a lot better off right now if only he'd listened. Then his eye settled on the guest room's massive mahogany rolltop desk, the property of some super-rich railroad baron of a century ago. Last time he'd slept here, he'd opened up that rolltop desk just for fun, and found it stuffed to overflowing with glossy eight-by-tens of gorgeous models and Hollywood starlets, many of them intimately inscribed to Mason with heartfelt testimonials to his sexual stamina or the size of his cock. Many still had resumés affixed to them, detailing bust, waist, and hip measurements, cup size, the color of hair and eyes. That night three years ago, practically on the eve of his marriage to Eugènie, Kevin had culled out a creamy green-eyed blonde, carried it into the bathroom with him, and come all over it.

"… out," said Jordan.

"What?"

"I said, stash your shit in the bureau, Kevin. My new secretary cooked us up a bowlful of chili. As soon as we've scarfed it, were going out."

CHAPTER 12

▼

A rectangular Judas hole blinked open in the massive oak door, and a man with a swarthy, pockmarked face eyed them warily from within. Then the door swung open on hand-forged hinges and Jordan led Kevin into the spacious high-walled adobe compound known as La Playa Azul. At the center of the compound, extending very nearly its entire length and width, was a miniature desert wilderness of stunted trees, cactuses, and flowering plants. An ochre flagstoned walkway wound through it, culminating, at odd intervals, in worn Spanish benches made of forged iron and weathered wood. A second walkway, this one paved with gray stones and wide enough for two people to walk abreast, encircled the open-air garden desert, serving as a kind of buffer between it and the establishment's thick, high, pale-blue stucco walls, with the clusters of small, pastel-colored cubicles—like the guest rooms in doll houses—nestled inside them. Full-bodied laughter and throaty moans wafted through the slatted wooden doors of the closed ones on whiffs of cigarette smoke, while in the open ones one spied a rumpled bed, a nightstand with wash basin, and a chest of drawers. On the paint-cracked wall above each bed gleamed a plastic crucifix, and tattered snapshots bristled from the dresser mirrors like porcupine quills. In one cubicle, with green walls and a single lightbulb suspended garishly from a knotted cord, a middle-aged Hispanic woman, her tie-dyed cotton dress hitched up ungracefully around her middle, squatted nonchalantly over her wash basin wash-ragging the area between her thighs.

Situated at wide intervals along the walls were much larger rooms, enterable through open archways, invariably choked with cigarette smoke, through each of which blared an outpouring of a wholly different variety of music, so that, standing outside, near the center of the compound, one was awash in a cacophonous miasma of sound.

"What did you say this place was called again?" asked Kevin.

"La Playa Azul," replied Jordan impatiently. "It means 'The Blue Beach.'"

"Why do they call it that?" inquired Kevin, but Jordan ignored him.

They entered one of the larger rooms, where a gold-toothed bartender in a soiled white jacket slouched lazily behind a modest bar while, close by, a half-dozen Hispanic musicians in well-worn suits hunched together on a ragged bandstand listlessly doling out medleys of Latin hits. In a wide-open area reserved for dancing, several couples danced, but there were neither many dancers, nor drinkers, presumably because it was only 10 PM on a Friday and the night was still young.

The whores, about a dozen of them, sat clustered around a clutch of card tables, opposite the band, whiling away their boredom in a desultory round-robin of pick-up-sticks.

The moment they spied Mason, however, the mood among the players brightened, and they clustered excitedly around him, like happy children around a maypole, hugging and kissing him and chirping ecstatic bilingual hellos. One player enthusiastically offered her seat, and Jordan gallantly accepted, stripping off his hand-tailored suede jacket and hanging it on the back of his chair.

"What's all this?" inquired Kevin.

"You already knew I was a fucking genius, right? Well, what you probably didn't know is that I am the world's fucking undisputed grand master of pick-up-sticks!"

"We came here to play pick-up-sticks?" exclaimed Kevin incredulously, but Jordan had already turned his mind to the game.

"*I* came here to play pick-up-sticks, my man," he answered finally over his shoulder. "You go get yourself a drink, score some shit, do whatever the fuck you want."

"Thanks," Kevin murmured, and ambled across the room toward the bar. For some reason, Kevin had never been able to abide the effects of alcohol. The most demure sip of white wine was enough to make his penis start tingling uncomfortably and then put him right to sleep. The near-instantaneous drowsiness, Kevin tended to ascribe to a simple lack of tolerance, but the discomfiting tingling sensation in his penis was a phenomenon even sagacious physicians had been at a loss to explain.

Fortunately, the bar was well stocked with soft drinks, including a subtly flavored apple soft drink that Kevin had once acquired a taste for during a brief trip to Mexico but had never been able to find in New York. His bottle of *manzanilla* now in hand, Kevin treated himself to a sip or two, and shambled toward the door. Jordan had evidently just executed some well-nigh-miraculous pick-up-sticks feat, and the gaming area erupted in raucous applause.

Out in the gray-stoned walkway, a man slumbered noisily in one of the many cotton hammocks slung outside the pastel cubicles, a pint of whiskey cradled affectionately in one hand, and Kevin saw a sloe-eyed hooker with wild, unkempt hair emerge from the cubicle closest by him perfunctorily smoothing her skirt.

Kevin turned left, strolling past a half-dozen other cubicles till he arrived at another of the larger, more public rooms, this one devoid of women, where men with hand-rolled cigarettes dangling precariously from their lips were silently embroiled in some obscure game like billiards played on an ancient table whose frayed felt covering was slick with grime and sweat.

Toward the back of the room, well clear of the billiard table, a dozen men were congregated raptly around a television set watching a continuous silent tape loop of a lanky Anglo farm boy, his denim coveralls bunched around his ankles, having sexual intercourse with a gigantic pig. The farm boy worked lackadaisically at his chosen task, his face expressionless, his eyes blank, as he socked it monotonously to the uncomplaining sow with unvarying thrusts of his bony hips.

The tape played on and on in an unvarying, unending loop, making it impossible, at least for Kevin, to discern where the tape ended and where it began. Yet none of that prevented the men from lapsing, without warning, into spontaneous gusts of uproarious guffaws, and always at the same exact moments, as though something hilarious had occurred on the tape which Kevin's eye could not see.

"Habla Anglais?" asked Kevin finally of one of the men.

"Bokito, si ... "

"What did you all find so funny just now?"

The man took a long, slow pull on his drink. He answered Kevin, even as his bloodshot eyes remained fixed on the screen: "Why for we are all laughing, is for the *estupido gringo* is fucking the peeg!"

Kevin drained the last sweet drops of his *manzanilla* and strolled back out to the walkway, circumnavigating the desert garden, peering curiously into a roomful of gimlet-eyed card players, and returning finally to the room with the pick-up-sticks contingent and the Latin band. A breathless hush had fallen over the pick-up-stickers as players and spectators alike joined forces in a silent, telekinetic attempt to levitate a seemingly indissoluble pick-up-sticks logjam so as to enable Mason to extract a clearly keystone stick without upsetting the precariously balanced equilibrium of the stack. Finally, however, after bringing to bear a valiant blend of yogi-like concentration and neurosurgical deftness—and after cannily milking the suspenseful situation for all it was worth—Jordan succeeded, and his gaggle of skimpily clad admirers erupted into an orgy of worshipful applause.

It was nearly midnight now, and the dance floor had begun to fill up. Through the open archway, Kevin watched as a great, black-haired bull of a man, clad only in undershorts and a gold crucifix, urinated indifferently on a five-foot-high cactus plant while a diminutive prostitute in a bright red hair ribbon pounded on his back with her fists.

Then a girl touched Kevin's arm and, in pleasant-sounding Spanish, asked him to dance with her. Kevin obliged her because, at that moment, the music was slow—a waltz, he thought, although, to be honest, he was not sure. Fast, unrestrained dancing was utterly beyond Kevin, even though, for as long as he could remember, he had always loved to stand on the sidelines and watch others throw themselves into it. Especially women. To watch a beautiful woman dancing with frenzied abandon was for Kevin this planet's most excruciatingly carnal spectacle. He would anchor himself to some safe object, like the back of a chair, and squeeze it till his knuckles showed white. And he would yearn to get up there and do it along with them, all the while knowing that if he were ever to turn himself loose in that way, ever to allow himself that kind and dimension of freedom, there was no question he would fuck them right there on the dance floor—no question he would grab them and tear their clothes off, no question he would hurl them to the floor and fuck them, no question that if he wasn't careful, he might even kill them. Even contemplating the possibility of it frightened Kevin to death.

By some mysterious, ethereal alchemy, the music had by now accelerated to foxtrot speed, but the whore was no longer in the mood for dancing. Now she wanted to fuck. She wore a tight black miniskirt and purple spike-heeled shoes and a black halter top. Rhinestones dangled from her earlobes like cheap chandeliers.

Her midriff was bare. Kevin's hand had been on it while they'd been dancing. Despite the closeness of the crowded room and the warmth of the night air, he had felt goose bumps there. The very thought of them was making him feel queasy. It occurred to him that another *manzanilla* might—but she was tugging insistently at him now, trying to coax—No, pull!—trying to *pull* him off the dance floor by force. With his free hand he clutched at her fingers, which clung unremittingly to his wrist with all the clammy tenacity of a rubber squid. She yammered away at him in Spanish as he pried them loose. His heart pounded and his mind reeled, trying to imagine what was going to happen next. *"MARICON!"* she spat, and turned on her heel and stormed away.

Sweating profusely, Kevin stumbled out into the courtyard and flung himself into the first hammock he saw. High, high above his head, the heavens were a churning ocean of storm-tossed rhinestone stars.

The next thing he knew, Jordan was towering over him, vigorously shaking him awake.

"Jesus Fucking H. Christ, Kevin! What in the holy fuck is the matter with you?"

"I must've gotten dragged out from my flight, Jordan. I guess I fell asleep."

"You are a major disappointment to me, my man. A fucking major, major disappointment. You could not get laid in a women's prison with a fistful of pardons. We all know that. But this is a fucking cathouse, old buddy, a fact which should be plain to all and sundry. And moreover, I was willing to put the *rite de passage* on my tab, old sock. If you can't get laid here—"

"Is the pick-up-sticks game over?"

"It is."

"And have you—"

"Have I what, Kevin?"

"Have—"

"If you're struggling to ask me whether I've gotten my rocks off yet, Kevin, the answer is no. Jordan Mason does not pay for his pussy, Kevin. Not here, not ever. Pussy comes to me, Kevin. It flows to me. You've seen the eight-by-tens in the desktop. I have to comb the pussy out of my teeth. I come here to play pick-up-sticks. Some of the girls are very good players. World class, no, but still very good. And of course I bring people here. Hollywood people. Friends. I have made some great deals here, Kevin. And, believe it or not, some of my most immortal creations have been born here, inspired by the endless hours of sitting in those folding chairs, playing at pick-up-sticks, awash in the aroma of Spanish gash."

"I want to go home, Jordan."

"You mean now? Tonight?"

"Tomorrow."

"For god's sake, why, Kevin? Don't tell me you're not having a good time!"

"I want to go home, Jordan. There's someone I—"

"Who, Kevin?"

"Someone."

"Good frigging god, Kevin! Don't tell me you yearn for a woman!"

CHAPTER 13

▼

Kevin thrust thirty dollars at the cashier in exchange for fifteen tokens and made an enthusiastic dash toward Vicki's booth. Eager to surprise her, he rolled a token into the coin slot and snatched up the phone. The booth's overhead lights blinked into darkness. The opaque black panel separating them whirred—and rose. Kevin gaped at her wide-eyed through the transparent partition and emitted a gasp of stunned disbelief.

"Who are you?" he stammered uncomprehendingly. "Where— where's Vicki?!"

In the starkly lit cubicle opposite him stood a scowling black giantess in a shimmering fuchsia spandex leotard, with a tempestuous black afro, iridescent scarab-beetle-green fingernails, and matching lipstick. Her left pinky had been fitted with a gleaming solid-gold fingernail, and a massive gold-plated earring in the shape of Africa swayed from each ear. Her breasts were as huge as plesiosaurs, and her gigantic aureoles, their outlines tautly etched by the skintight leotard, spread out across the forbidding landscape of her bosom like a pair of enveloping purple circus tents.

"Screw where Vicki's at!" she snapped. "Lemme see you whip out your pecker—assumin', that is, y'all got any kind of a pecker to whip out!"

Kevin froze in horror. Gold teeth snicker-snacked inside her head like torturous implements. A faceted diamond nestled inside one of her incisors usurped wattage from the garish booth lights and bedazzled him like the glare of some alien sun.

"Vicki," he barely whispered. "I'm—"

"You hear me what I'm tellin' you, boy?" she commanded imperiously. "I be's tellin' you to pull out your god damned dick!"

Kevin obeyed her wordlessly, fumblingly unzipping his fly, reaching inside his jockey shorts, showing her his flaccid penis in the palm of his hand.

"Now watch it," she admonished him sternly, plunging her ham hands into her scoop neck and grasping a breast in each hand, "'cause I'm 'bout to do you somethin' ain't 'bout to get done to you nowheres else!"

And with that she wrenched her breasts free and squeezed, squirting the plexiglass with twin sprays of milk.

Kevin was aghast.

"You better had toke it up in a hurry, peewee," crackled her voice over the telephone. "That damn shit wall's 'bout to close down."

Kevin released his hold on his penis and dropped a second token into the slot. His heart skipped a beat as the eel-like surface of her tongue suddenly appeared on the plexiglass, swirling obscenely across its surface, licking a moist swath through the milk.

"Shee-yit, peewee!" The diamond incisor glistened like a serpent's eye. "Don't tell me you ain't gonna *do* nothing!"

"Do what?"

"Ain't too awfully much they *don't* do, honey! Pound they pud sometimes and scarf it off the glass, sometimes crap into a paper cup and then like for me to watch 'em eat it. But—"

"Vicki!" gasped Kevin, trying not to vomit. "I'm—"

"I ain't good enough for you, is that it? Is that what you be sayin'?"

"No," stammered Kevin, choking. "It's just—"

"Forget it, you peewee asshole! Just tell me—how many of them damn tokes y'all got left?"

Kevin thrust out his sweaty, bulging fist.

"Hmm! Seems to be 'bout twelve. Okay, you go jam 'em in the— no, wait, never you mind. You be seein' that crack where the plastic window meets the floor? S'pose you just slide 'em on under there, one by one."

"But—"

"Damn it, you little fucker! Will you do what you been told?"

She squatted down and avariciously snatched them up as Kevin meekly slid them through the crack. She was still busily at it when the forbidding black panel began to descend.

"Hey, wait a minute!" exclaimed Kevin frantically. "Where—"

The black panel had all but completely descended now. In the absence of the light from the slut's side, Kevin abruptly became aware of the rapidly enveloping darkness. "Wait! Tell me—"

"It be's her day off today," proclaimed the oracular voice of the serpent tooth, eerily disembodied now in the darkness. "Prob'ly, she be's back here tomorrow."

CHAPTER 14

▼

Kevin inserted his ChemBank card into the cash machine and deftly keyed in S-H-M-B-L-R, his six-letter pass-code for the past ten years. To guard against overspending, Kevin had begun withdrawing small amounts of cash only as he needed it, nibbling away at his checking account in weekly hundred-dollar bites. He touched the portion of the video display marked CHECKING ACCOUNT, then the one marked WITHDRAWAL, and pecked in the one-hundred-dollar amount. The machine hemmed and harrumphed the way Eugènie had whenever he'd asked for sex, invariably requiring some painstaking interlude in which to process his request. At least with the machine you always knew what the answer would be. At least the machine didn't demand that you whip out your dick.

SORRY. YOUR TRANSACTION CANNOT BE COM-PLETED. YOUR WITHDRAWAL LIMIT HAS BEEN EXCEEDED.

Mumbling "fuck" under his breath, Kevin cleared the display screen and tried it again.

SORRY. YOUR TRANSACTION CANNOT BE COM-PLETED. YOUR WITHDRAWAL LIMIT HAS BEEN EXCEEDED.

He tried it a third time, but the robot teller remained obdurate. Kevin cleared the display screen, called up the accounts display, and tried to tap into the mother lode of his savings account. The machine whirred superciliously, serenely smug in being essential to others' needs while lacking any needs of its own.

SORRY, it chortled sadistically. YOUR TRANSACTION CAN-NOT BE—

Kevin slammed the cancellation button, yanked back his plastic card, and charged through the glass doorway separating the room with the automatic cash machines from the rest of the bank. It was just after twelve noon on a Friday, the neighborhood branch was clogged with patrons, and of course the majority of the tellers and bank officers were out to lunch. Kevin dutifully waited on line at the service desk while scenarios of mayhem and carnage surged through his head.

"And how may I help you today, sir?" inquired the gaunt Irish spinster, who had raised to a high art the practice of striding back and forth across the bank with seeming purposefulness during the logjam hours waving a single, meaningless scrap of paper in her hand.

"Well," began Kevin, "the automatic cash—"

"Account number?" she snapped.

Kevin handed her the numbers of both accounts and watched her nimbly click-clack the integers into her countertop terminal, her pointy nose wrinkling and raptorlike eyes narrowing as the ebb and flow of his finances danced on the screen.

"You'd like me to close these out for you permanently, sir?"

"Close—? No, I'd like to make a with—"

"Nice trick if you can do it, sir. There are no funds in these accounts."

"What?"

"They're empty."

"Empty?"

"Dry as the proverbial—"

"But how? That's not possible! I had—"

"A creditor, sir. Someone evidently presented the bank with a valid—"

"That's preposterous! A valid what? I don't—"

"A judgment, sir."

"But I had close to twelve thou—"

"Your monthly activity statement was mailed out on Monday, sir. Un—"

"Who?"

"Sir?"

"Who the hell took my money?"

The Irish woman who had never known the act of love smiled wanly at him and shrugged.

"WHO?"

"We do not have that information here, sir. But if you'll fill out this yellow form, and have it notarized, our main—"

"WHO IN THE GOD DAMN HELL STOLE MY MONEY??"

"There are other people waiting, sir."

Kevin pounded on the countertop.

The Gaelic vulture rolled her eyes.

A sullen murmur went up from the throng at the service desk, and Kevin was not at all certain it was sympathetic toward him. A somnolent rent-a-cop, roused from his habitual lethargy by the threatening mood of the crowd, was buttoning his uniform jacket over his protuberant potbelly and striding purposefully toward him. Striving as best he could to maintain the illusion of dignity, Kevin snatched up the proffered bank form and retreated swiftly out the door.

There wasn't anyone in the world Kevin owed money to. Not anyone. One of his little fetishes was to pay all his bills the same day he received them. He never—

Then, suddenly, Kevin flashed on the divorce agreement, the only thing in his life involving serious bucks. There'd been a lump sum payable to Eugènie when the divorce was finalized, and although he'd practically choked on it, he'd managed to pay it on time. And then, of course, there were monthly mortgage payments due at the bank, but he'd paid them punctually—albeit reluctantly—every time.

It was springtime, and the girls strolling down Columbus Avenue looked fabulous. It was great to be single and to be able to stare at them unabashedly everywhere one went. He had treated himself to a *Little Nemo* book a month ago and put it on his Visa card, but that was only sixty-five dollars and he'd paid that bill the day it came in. And besides, what the hell was he doing agonizing over this petty bullshit for anyway? He could've let his bills stack up for months and they still wouldn't have amounted to twelve thousand bucks. And didn't they have to at least notify you before they stole your bank account?

He went back to his apartment and dialed Eugènie. Actually, all he had to do was press a button and the automatic-dialing gizmo hooked up to his telephone did all the rest. Ron Hinder had given it to him when he'd first moved in here, along with an instruction booklet on how to program it with up to a dozen of his most frequently dialed numbers. Nowadays, Kevin hardly ever talked to Eugènie at all, but he'd long since misplaced the instruction booklet and so couldn't remember how to delete her number from the program and key in the number of someone else.

"Hello?"

"Eugènie, it's me, Kevin. I'm—"

"Kevin?"

"I'm really sorry to bother you, Eugènie, but I'm trying to cope with a minor—it probably has nothing to do with you, but I thought—"

"What?"

"I've just come from the bank. They say some creditor cleaned out my checking and savings accounts. I know it's probably just some—"

"You think I did it?"

"No, of course not. I didn't mean that. It's just some kind of mistake. Only I swear I don't owe anybody any money. The only halfway heavy financial obligation I have has to—"

"You mean our divorce?"

"Uh-huh."

There was a discomfiting pause on her end which Kevin did not understand.

"You don't owe me any money, Kevin, except—"

"The house, which I've—"

"Yes, of course you have." She paused again. "What about Arthur?"

"Arthur?"

"Have you paid Arthur?"

"Arthur?"

"The papers you took home with you that day, Kevin. Remember?"

"Papers?"

"You took them home with you? To reread them? Don't you—"

"Those papers?"

"You reread them, right? Before you signed them and sent them in?"

"I—I don't remember."

"That's why you said you wanted them." She sounded awfully nervous. "To look them over before you—"

"But that was just the property agreement," interjected Kevin. "The house. The—"

"And Arthur's fees."

Kevin would have liked to repeat the words, but they remained clogged in his larynx like a clump of lead.

"Kevin?"

"Arthur's—"

"Fees. Part of the divorce settlement was that you agreed to pay Arthur's fees."

"We discussed that?!"

"I'm sure we must've. Anyway, it's—"

"In the agreement."

"Right. In the agreement."

"Thanks, Eugènie."

"Hey, listen, I'm—"

Kevin hung up the receiver gently, taking the utmost care not to slam it. He went to his file cabinet, pulled out the divorce agreement, and flipped through it till he reached the final page: "... in addition," proclaimed the fateful words, "Defendant agrees to pay Plaintiff's attorney's fees in the amount of twelve thousand five hundred seventy-five dollars ($12,575) within sixty.... Failure to make such timely payment shall entitle...."

The telephone jangled, jarring Kevin back into the workaday world. It was his mother, inviting him over for a home-cooked meal. He accepted gladly, but there must have been something in the sound of his voice, because she responded by asking him if something was wrong. Yes, there was, he admitted, adding that he'd talk it over with her when he got there.

Then he hung up the phone and brought down all his porcelain marmalade jars from the kitchen cabinet, setting them out on the formica countertop near the sink. He unscrewed all five lids, then poured out the contents and began to count—but even before he'd begun, he knew almost exactly what the final total would be, because each jar was brimful, and that meant each one contained about fifty-four dollars in quarters. It was an old custom he'd maintained since childhood, that of emptying out his pockets at the end of the day and saving the coins in one particular denomination in jars. He'd begun with pennies as a boy, leap-frogged to dimes, and finally settled on quarters about the time he dropped out of school. Periodically, some mini-crisis occurred that necessitated rolling the coins into paper rolls and lugging them to the bank.

But there'd never been a financial crisis quite like this one, and Kevin knew that with his writing income nonexistent and his savings account gone, the approximately two hundred and seventy dollars he had in quarters wasn't likely to last for very long.

Kevin shaved, dressed, sifted lackadaisically through a stack of newly arrived comics, then caught a crosstown bus to his mother's home on the Upper East Side. All of the doormen knew him, and always waved him by, and whenever a new man came on duty who might not recognize him, his mom always took care to advise the new man he was coming, so he wouldn't be stopped in the lobby while they called upstairs.

She was waiting for him when he got off the elevator, wearing some godawful hunk of junk jewelry he'd bought her as a present when he was seven years old. "How can you wear that?" he asked her. "Why shouldn't I wear it?" she laughed. "I think it's adorable!"

The apartment was large, very large in comparison to the dwellings available to most members of Kevin's generation, with a spacious foyer, opulent living and dining rooms, a sunlit kitchen, and three large bedrooms off the long main hall.

Kevin's parents had moved here from Teaneck when he was a senior in high school, so Kevin had actually only lived here for seven or eight months before packing up his belongings and flying off to Ann Arbor, Michigan, to attend the university there, while his sister, Ora, who was six years younger, had remained behind to attend a snooty private school in Manhattan, spending her summers and holidays zipping around Europe and the Middle East on her father's credit card, before relocating to Pennsylvania to major in art history and hard-hat feminism at Bryn Mawr. Her bedroom, adjoining his parents', remained faithfully preserved just as she'd left it—her early-American canopied bed with its hand-sewn patchwork quilt, her framed and mounted display of autographs of famous women artists, her menagerie of stuffed animals, perkily propped up in an antique doll cradle and preciously poised in eternal anticipation of their mistress's return—while Kevin's former bedroom, just a few strides down the hall, had been made over completely shortly following his departure to provide space where his father could work without leaving home.

Indeed, the principal motive for leaving Teaneck in the first place had been to enable Kevin's dad to do all the things he loved to do without his having to go too far to do them: the ballet, the opera, the fine-art museums, even the marathon runners crossing the finish line in

Central Park—all these manifold pleasures were no more than the briefest cab ride away.

Now, strolling down the long hallway to the living room, and then cutting through it to the dining room just beyond, Kevin paused to take in the sundry accumulations and assemblages that seemed to exemplify his life: the rare first editions and antique inkwells, the shelves lined with classical records, the Lilliputian bronze cavalry of Hindu temple toys posed stern and mute by the fireplace. Most self-expressive of all, however, were the scores of nineteenth-century drawings and watercolors, scrupulously matted in vintage antique frames: the pastel-shaded renderings of rustic rural villages and farmland, thatch-roofed cottages and vineyards and verdant landscapes, that together comprised a kind of pastoral fantasy montage reflecting his father's wistful yearnings of escape from the maddening confinements of a shut-in's life.

"He did enjoy the stories I used to bring him, didn't he, Ma?"

Kevin and his mother were seated across from one another at the candlelit polished-mahogany dining-room table, in the same places they'd always sat, the ornate, vacant armchair at the head of the table dominating the evening as a redwood tree might, or a ghost.

"Of course he did, Kev. I know he did."

"But you don't mind my asking?"

"Of course not. Why would I mind?"

"It's been eight months. I haven't been able to write a line since the day he died."

"And you think—"

"That?"

"—that there may be some sort of—"

"Only that I always thought of myself as writing my stories as gifts for him. And now that he's—"

"Kevin," interjected his mother quietly, "I don't—"

As a writer of comic books, Kevin earned his livelihood writing dialogue. He had an expert's ear for spoken language, and his instincts for

the rhythms of conversation were finely honed. People generally interrupted one another when they conversed, but not his mother. If now
she had chosen to cut him off in mid-sentence, it was because she had
something important to say.

"—know if this will be of any help to you, Kevin. And I know
you're a sensitive person and so this may hurt your feelings. But it may
also help you to get a closer perspective on what seems to have become
a troubling situation for you."

"Okay…"

"Your father loved you very much. You were his pride and joy. He
was disappointed when you chose to drop out of Michigan, most parents of our generation would be, but he remained extraordinarily
proud of you and supportive of your ambition to become a writer."

"Is there a 'but' coming?"

"But people have their limitations, Kevin. A big part of life is learn-
ing how to cope with and understand the limitations of others. When
your father was a boy, comic books weren't valued as the vital popular
American art form they're seen as today. They were the things
lower-class kids read, draftees, junk. Your father had a huge falling out
with *his* father when he went away to college and announced his refusal
to study Greek. Grandpa never forgave him for it, and, in some ways,
despite his accomplishments, your father never forgave himself either.
He felt just a little bit inferior, all his adult life, just because he didn't
know—"

"Greek?"

"Greek."

"But the fact that grandpa had treated him that way about Greek,
didn't that—"

"No, it didn't. Because some lessons just don't sink in. So if he was
not quite as enthusiastic about your stories as you would have liked
him to be, or if you somehow received conflicting signals from him of
being pleased and proud on the one hand but still a little let down and
disappointed on the other, you've just got to try to take it in stride. It

was his limitation, his shortcoming, not yours. Even the people in this world who love us the most aren't going to love every single thing about us. It's just a fact of life you've got to accept somehow, and move on."

"Okay."

"You think it may help?"

Kevin shrugged. "I don't know."

"I love your comic book stories. I adored the Shambler. I can't wait to—"

"Okay."

"Okay?"

"Enough. Thanks."

"Okay, good. And now unless you're going to help yourself to a third slice of that pie, I've got something I've been meaning to give you."

"What?"

"This way."

They rose from the table and traversed the long hallway, past what had once been his bedroom, then past Ora's room, till they arrived at his parents' room, close by the foyer, nearest the front door. Kevin's mother had been in the process of redecorating this room when his father died, and his mother still had not recouped the spiritual resources needed to complete the task, and so it remained as she had left it, unfinished, with a medley of wallpaper swatches scotch-taped to the wall, a trio of paint samples tacked to a baseboard, and a hideous lighting fixture hung in place but not yet connected, its wiring askew. Nonetheless, her seemingly infinite capacity for rejuvenation and renewal never ceased to amaze him—even as he so often sulked in the shadows of the past, wanting only for things to remain the same.

The bedroom featured two walk-in closets, one of them the sanctum sanctorum of his father, who used to undress there in the evenings prior to taking his nightly bath. As Kevin's mother stepped to the closet and swung the door open, it occurred to Kevin that he hadn't seen the inside of that closet in years.

"You remember those colorful wool-flannel shirts he always liked to wear because they made him feel as though he were out for a walk in the woods?"

"You bet."

"There are three or four of them in here somewhere. Remember how you always used to compliment him on them? I think there are one or two brand-new ones he never even wore."

A long pole for hanging clothes ran down the left-hand side of the closet; an elaborate shelf unit, including a special rack for shoes, was built into the wall at the right. Between them, at the far end of the closet, stood a large chest of drawers. Kevin's mother was up on a low stool now, squinting through the sides of the half-dozen or so large translucent plastic boxes stacked on a top shelf. "This may take a minute," she said.

Standing proudly atop the oak dresser was a gigantic color photograph of Kevin's sister in an ornate gilt frame, surrounded by other, smaller photographs of her—astride a dromedary in Egypt, backpacking in France, capped and gowned for her Bryn Mawr graduation, hoisting a giant banner at a rally for the E.R.A.—in frames of sundry sizes and shapes.

"Here they are," trilled his mother. "I'll be down in a second."

Crayon drawings made by his sister in grade school were still tacked to the shelving. There was a sampler she'd made, featuring a wide-eyed little girl with a grotesquely smiling face. On a chest-high shelf, Kevin spied a trio of tiny snapshots—one of his mother, one of his sister, one that looked like the wallet-sized version of the graduation photo taken for his high-school yearbook—all encased in a triple frame. In the entire closet, damn it if it wasn't the only—

"It's a delightful picture of you," volunteered his mother cheerfully, reading his mind.

"Terrific," smiled Kevin wanly, turning, plunging his hands in his pockets as he extricated himself from the shrine. His mother followed him, bearing a small stack of brightly colored yet manly outdoor shirts, producing a plastic shopping bag, slipping them inside. "They'll fit you perfectly," she reassured him. And Kevin accepted them, like a man being asked to spend a night in a leper's clothes.

It was time to go. Outside in the hallway, she touched his arm. "Kev, over the phone you said you had a problem. Was that it, about Dad liking the stories?"

Kevin nodded. Some imbecile was holding the elevator captive way up on the ninth floor. The plastic shopping bag was starting to sweat in his arm.

Would it help you get over this rough spot, Kev, if I lent you a few hundred dollars? If you're experiencing such difficulty working—"

Kevin fixed her with a taut smile and shook his head.

Finally, the elevator came and he rode it down to the lobby and strode out the door. He tossed the shirts in the first refuse basket he came to and rode home on the crosstown bus. He only hoped the sanitation department came by and collected the garbage before his mother walked out of her building and spotted them lying there.

CHAPTER 15

▼

The cashier accepted Kevin's roll of quarters with a sullenly disdainful expression and begrudgingly handed over five hexagonal tokens in exchange. Vicki's booth was occupied, and so Kevin waited, more cautious than last time, until her current patron departed and she stepped back out onto the rotunda to strut her stuff.

She spotted him almost immediately, and for an instant their eyes met. Her blue eyes sparkled and her complexion glowed as though lit from within. Nonetheless, it always made Kevin uneasy when women seemed to glow, since he was never sure whether it was his feelings for them that caused the glow, or theirs for him.

Inside the booth, he released his tokens eagerly into the coin slot, his heady elation undiminished by the iron finality with which they thudded home. When the booth lights dimmed, and the panel rose, she stood there facing him in tight-fitting sea-green shorts and a matching halter, her blond curls freshly peroxided, her smile the sultry color of blood.

"I've really missed you," he whispered hoarsely into the mouthpiece.

"Hey! I know! So what've you been up to?"

"I was in New Mexico. I just got back."

"Writing comic books, right?"

"No, R and R."

"What?"

"Just goofing off. Hanging out." He wondered if he should tell her about the Playa Azul.

"Hey, works for me, right?"

"I thought I saw you at the airport."

"You did?!"

"In Albuquerque. You—"

"Albuquerque?"

"You were wearing a—"

"But it wasn't me, Kevin. It's Kevin, right?"

"Yes, that's—"

"It wasn't me you—"

"Yes, I know that. But I wanted it to be."

An amused look flitted across her face, and a smile.

Kevin rushed on. "I came here practically from the airport. No, I came here from the airport, and I—"

"You mean, right here?"

Kevin nodded. "And I got—"

"Shana?" she giggled. "Shana the She-Devil?"

"Shana the—"

"Those trashy green fingernails? Gazungas down to the linoleum?"

Kevin was grinning like an idiot. He started to say—

"Oh god! How gross! And did—did she flip them out and—"

"Yes," Kevin was nodding frantically. "Yes, yes."

"And did she—" Vicki was laughing and giggling. "Oh god! How gross!"

Kevin began laughing, too.

"We have got to get you into sex, Kevin."

"Hunh—?!"

"You heard me."

"Yes. Okay. But I don't—"

"So that you'll keep coming back here."

"I'll keep coming back, Vicki," whispered Kevin reverently.

He'd barely completed the sentence when she unhooked her skimpy halter and let it fall to the ground. Her breasts were firm yet delicate, the nipples a faintly blushing, unprepossessing pink. Kevin felt—

"You're not one of those assholes who're totally hung up on size, are you, Kevin?"

Kevin shook his head.

"You're not about to—"

He abruptly glanced at his wristwatch, all at once fearful that he might run out of time."

"—give me some kind of shitty—"

In the fragile aura of light glowing faintly through the plexiglass from her side of the booth, Kevin could make out that he had barely two and a half minutes left.

"Vicki!" he exclaimed urgently. "You're beautiful! But, please, listen to me! I've got some things I—"

"I've never seen your thing, Kevin, remember?"

"Vicki, lis—"

"I'll bet you showed it to—"

"Please listen!"

"Hey, okay, don't get—"

"I don't want to leave without apologizing."

"Huh-!?"

"For last time."

"What—"

"I got really annoyed with you for those things you said to me about my father hating comic books. I prob—"

"I said?"

"I was unpleasant. And I'm sorry. You were right. He did. It's given me a whole new perspective. I'm sorry."

"Forget it. I don't even remem—"

"And there's another thing. It's complicated and it has to do with my divorce and there isn't time to explain it. Bur right now I'm broke.

I mean, until I can straighten all this out and finish unraveling all this bullshit about my—"

"I don't get any of this. What—"

"I need to be able to see you, Vicki. You're the only one who's sane who I can talk to about this stuff, the only person in my entire life who seems to—"

"Me?!"

"God damn it, Vicki, they took my bank account. Two hundred and fifty dollars in quarters is all I've got left."

"Oh god!"

"If you'd just help me get through this. Till I can get this craziness behind me and turn in the Cicada. I mean there must be something you could do, some way you could fix it, so that I can come in here, and we can talk, without my having to put all those damn tokens in."

"You don't mean—"

"Yes?"

"—you want me to see you for free, Kevin?"

"I'd pay you back, Vicki. I swear, I'd pay double. I'd pay you back double. If—"

Without warning, the black panel had begun its descent. Kevin first became aware of it not as an intruding object, but as a darkening shadow ominously cutting off his light.

"VICKI!"

"Kevin, I'm sorry, but I don't know. I'd like to Kevin. You're a really great—"

The shadow had already obscured her face, her neck. Now it plunged inexorably downward to slice off her breasts.

"—guy, so I'd like to. But my boss. The manage—"

Kevin blundered forward, obsessed with somehow braking the black panel's downward glide at least until he'd won the few precious moments he needed to reason with her, talk with her, win her over to his point of view. Only in mid-lunge did it come home to him that the swiftly descending panel was on her side of the transparent wall panel, not his, and that there was no way on earth that he could stop it. In that bemused, beclouded instant, it dawned on him that he might not have been out of time at all, that she'd somehow triggered the panel's descent prematurely just to get rid of him. And then suddenly, as he thrust his palms forward to cushion his impact against the booth wall, the fingertips of his right hand somehow acquired a fragile purchase beneath an exposed edge of the transparent plexiglass wall panel where the plywood of the booth and the plexiglass met. The black panel had all but completely descended now, and Kevin's booth had been plunged into pitch darkness except for a thin knife edge of light. In that volatile instant of rage and disorientation, Kevin tore back hard, wrenching nearly the entire plexiglass wall panel loose from the wall. The black panel had descended completely now, and the booth lights were on, but Kevin's vision was obscured by the swirling morass of plaster and peeling paint fragments dislodged from the booth's ceiling and winnowing down from overhead.

Kevin's hearing registered the alarm's piercing shriek without his fully comprehending what it was. Then the flimsy inside latch flew off the booth door and two brawny pairs of arms—one white, one black— dragged him out of the tiny room. The black pair belonged to the house cashier who'd regarded Kevin's roll of quarters with undisguised contempt.

Kevin had to laugh. In its interracial aspect, after all, wasn't it just like comic books—where an unwritten but nonetheless religiously observed rule stipulated that no villainous or criminal act could be committed by blacks unless it was perpetrated in concert with equally villainous whites?

The two bouncers dragged Kevin across the rotunda and down the long flight of stairs to the street.

"Weird-ass lump of shit!" snarled one.

"Crazy fucked-up asshole!" opined his friend.

Then they seized Kevin by the arms and legs and hurled him across the sidewalk into the street.

"Don't come back," advised one of them, "or we'll tear off your motherfucking head and puke in it!"

CHAPTER 16

▼

Resplendent in his aquamarine turban and tunic of ornate crimson brocade, the bearded Hindu colossus swung open the elaborately metal-worked bronze door, ushering Kevin and his lunchtime companion, the Dragon Lady, into the sumptuously appointed expense-account caravansary known as the Mumtaz Mahal. A gigantic mural of elephant-mounted maharajahs on a tiger hunt dominated the dining room, and ceiling-recessed spotlights pinpointed wall niches adorned with sculptures of opulently bosomed Hindu goddesses, some of them evidently quite ancient and therefore lacking an arm or a leg or a head.

Then, of a sudden, their Hindu giant gestured, and lo, from out of nowhere, materialized a somewhat lesser giant—this one attired in a lavender turban and white brocade—to guide them to the very epicenter of this lush oasis and seat them at a table set with gold-plated flatware and goblets so huge that one could effortlessly drown oneself if the business deal under discussion did not turn out well.

Even at this early juncture, Kevin noted, the portents were such as did not bode well. The Dragon Lady was well known to have year-round simultaneous lunchtime reservations at two posh restaurants, the Mumtaz Mahal and Club Eleven, both of them a bare stone's throw from Dynamic Comics, and the establishment to which she elected to bring you proved generally to be a reliable harbinger of your fate. Success attended those fortunate enough to dine at Club Eleven, where the location of one's table and the effusiveness, or lack thereof, of the maître d's welcome served as unvarying indices of a patron's prestige and power, while humiliation and disaster usually lay in wait at the Mumtaz Mahal, where the menu actually had prices on it and where the too-liberally spiced victuals scorched the living bejesus out of your throat.

At seventy, the Dragon Lady was still an austerely handsome, even beautiful, woman, with long silver-gray hair—which she wore either folded into a chignon or in a single braid nearly down to her waist— and pale blue eyes that could bore through your pretensions like augurs of ice. She was partial to gracefully flowing, brightly colored dresses, not business suits—sufficiently sedate not to transmit a misleading signal, yet not infrequently brightened by a dash of whimsy—which served to forcefully remind you that she had not always been old, on the one hand, and also to express her disdain for the austerely unisex uniforms that sterile designers had foisted upon an entire younger generation of career women desperate to be taken seriously as they stressed for success.

The daughter of an affluent Boston neurosurgeon and art collector, the Dragon Lady had attended college at Wellesley and precipitated a family scandal when, at the tender, headstrong age of seventeen, she made a private weekend pilgrimage to the Milford, Connecticut, home of America's most celebrated poet laureate and stayed on there as his mistress for the next fifteen years. A half-dozen of his finest poems bear florid testimony to the insatiable vigor of her sex drive, if not exactly her nurturing temperament, and his last three volumes of poetry were all admiringly dedicated to her.

Three or four years following his death, the Dragon Lady landed a job—reputedly as a by-product of her torrid extramarital liaison with the board chairman of Temp Worldwide Enterprises, which owned Dynamic Magazines, Inc.—as Dynamic's director of circulation, with a mandate to find ways to attract female readers to comics to help reverse the calamitous downward spiral of sales that had haunted the entire industry since the close of World War II.

The affair with the board chairman soon ended, and the attempt to erect a female readership base foundered, but that did not prevent the Dragon Lady from succeeding, by dint of innovative brilliance and hard work, from stemming the sales decline and initiating a steady upward trend. Promoted to publisher, then vice-president, and finally president, all in the face of frequently spiteful male intransigence, she capped her tenth anniversary with Dynamic by spearheading a buyout of Dynamic from its parent corporation and changing its name from Dynamic Magazines, Inc., to Dynamic Comics.

Her celebrated energy and decisiveness notwithstanding, however, the leadership characteristic that most distinguished the Dragon Lady was without doubt her idiosyncratic management style. She disdained formal meetings, and with the exception of her administrative assistant, even her closest subordinates seldom spoke with her. Months went by during which the company was guided almost entirely by nuggets of wisdom gleaned from memos she had dictated years ago in response to entirely different situations, or on the basis of offhand remarks she made to young secretaries and production assistants she encountered by sheer chance in the ladies' room.

Undeniably the most renowned such episode occurred after she casually confided to an awed eighteen-year-old pasteup girl that the plethora of yellow dresses introduced that spring was making her ill, an inauspicious *bon mot* that resulted in the virtual overnight elimination of the disapproved color from all forty of Dynamic's monthly comic book covers and serious editorial consideration of banishing it altogether from the insides. Only two years later, after the Dragon Lady had worn a bright yellow blouse to the office, was the ban on yellow lifted and its place in the colorist's palette restored.

"I really appreciate your giving me this time," volunteered Kevin respectfully. "I know—"

"I don't want you to give that a moment's thought, Kevin. You've been one of our most prodigious, most productive writers for—"

"Not lately," he confessed. "Not—"

She lifted her giant goblet to her lips and sipped her water.

"—for the past eight months. For the past eight months—"

The waiter arrived and took their order. The names of the exotic Indian entrées danced about the menu in a kind of dyslexic blur.

"For the past eight months—"

"But the Silver Cicada, Kevin," she interrupted him. "A memo from Ron Hinder crossed my desk just the other day, saying that—"

"That?"

"That you'd come in with some wonderfully innovative ideas on that project, and that it was just—"

"I have been working on it," blurted Kevin. "Very hard. And I think I've come up with some damn fine ideas for it. But—"

"But?"

"—something's missing. Something I can't get a handle on. Something that'll make—"

She coughed impatiently. "Hinder's memo promised we'd be receiving the first few plots and an overview almost any—"

"It's all my fault, not Hinder's. He knows I'm having trouble. He's trying to protect me, keep me out of the dog house. I'd feel awful if you blamed—"

"Don't worry about Ron Hinder, Kevin. He's the most solid editor I've got. And don't worry about the memo either. I shouldn't even have mentioned it. Editors are supposed to run interference for their freelancers from time to time. It's part of their job description. Freelancers conspiring with their editors to outwit the management is practically the essence of good publishing. If I pretend not to notice it, more often than not it's just that, pretending. But the question for us to face here and now is why—"

"I don't know why. I just know that I haven't been able to write anything in the last eight months. Eugènie and I were all involved in getting a divorce. There was all—"

"Divorce? I didn't—"

"It's not the divorce." Kevin chewed his lip. "It's something else. My father passed away eight months ago. I haven't been able to write a line since the—"

The waiter arrived with the food, and while he adroitly served up the dishes, the conversation stopped. Kevin took a forkful of curry, blew on it gently, and lifted it tentatively to his mouth—only to withdraw it hastily when his lower lip smouldered into a conflagration no amount of water would put out. The Dragon Lady, by sharp contrast, came from the Planet of Androids and no mere earthly tribulation could cause her pain.

"You see some viable connection, then, between—"

"Yes, I do," interjected Kevin. "My father and I were very close, and I think that, however he may have felt about them, I used to write my stories as gifts for him. And with—"

Kevin could have sworn he saw the Dragon Lady wince.

"And with him gone—"

"You've never been in psychotherapy of any kind, have you, Kevin?"

Kevin shook his head.

"Well, I have been. I was in psychoanalysis five days a week for the better part of eighteen years, and there's a guiding principle I've drawn from that experience that I would like to share with you. Quite simply, it is that when attempting to illuminate your own motives in a painful and complex psychological situation, the surest way to inner truth is to embrace the least palatable explanation you can think of, the one that places you in the least favorable light."

"I'm sorry," stammered Kevin apologetically, "but I don't think I—"

"You say you and your father were close, and that you thought of the comic book stories you wrote as gifts for him. But you also imply that your father may have had mixed feelings about those gifts. So let's try pursuing that tack awhile. Let's assume for the moment that, like most upper-middle-class adults of his generation, your father was contemptuous of comics. No matter how graciously he may have tried to behave when you presented him with your stories, the last thing in the world he wanted was a son who'd devoted his life to the creation of junk. And on some level you intuited this. You knew it to be true. Seen in this light, then, your so-called 'gifts' were hardly acts of love at all. On the contrary, they were acts of animus and hatred. How else to characterize a steady stream of gifts that you know make the recipient unhappy and that he does not want?" The Dragon Lady paused to take a sip of water. "Are you following me so far?"

Kevin blinked at her, saying nothing. But his eyes were burning and his mouth was dry.

"So here you are, month after month, churning out stories that, on some inaccessible level, are actually expressions of unconscious hatred toward your father. And then finally—"

"Finally?"

"—he dies. The murderous unconscious fantasy of killing your father comes true. Or, rather, it seems to come true. He would have died anyway, of course. Your stories had nothing whatever to do with it. But the fantasy is that they did. That you *killed* him. The feelings of remorse, the guilt, are overwhelming. Paralyzing. So you punish yourself for your heinous crime by depriving yourself of your livelihood. You must never be allowed to write another story lest, by chance, you kill again."

"You believe that?" inquired Kevin incredulously.

The Dragon Lady shrugged. "They haven't given me a license to practice yet," she said.

"It sounds completely crazy," exclaimed Kevin.

The Dragon Lady had returned to her Indian food and was assaulting it with gusto. If she started to choke while eating it, Kevin was fearful he wouldn't know how to execute the Heimlich maneuver.

"It sounds insane!"

The Dragon Lady was sopping up her chickpeas with one of those weird floppy wafers of Indian bread.

"I didn't hate my father! I adored my father!"

"I'm going to have to start thinking about getting back to the office soon, Kevin," remarked the Dragon Lady, glancing at her diamond watch. "What is it exactly you—"

"I'm in kind of an unexpected bind," began Kevin awkwardly. "I was hoping you, Dynamic, might—"

"Why don't you go back up to the office and voucher the first few Cicada plots, Kevin. That way we'll have a check waiting for you the moment you turn them in."

"I don't like coming to you like this," pleaded Kevin. "Please believe me, I don't like it at all. It's not that I haven't been working on the Cicada. I have been. I've been working on it hard. But I'm in this slump. And I'll work myself out of it, I know I will. I just—"

"What?"

"Some extra help. Just—"

"What is it exactly you're asking for, Kevin?"

"An advance of some kind. A loan." Kevin sucked in his breath. "Something—I was hoping—ten thousand dollars. Or maybe a draw. Just for three or four months. Say, twenty-five—"

"I can't get into this with you, Kevin."

"I've been working for Dynamic for nearly thirteen years," whispered Kevin softly, his voice quavering. "I've written over four hundred—"

"And Dynamic has paid you for those stories, Kevin. Every one of them. And whenever we've reprinted any of them, we've paid you reprint money. When we've succeeded in licensing characters you've created, we've paid you a percentage. I think we've conscientiously fulfilled all our obligations to you throughout those thirteen years, don't you, Kevin?"

"Yes, of course, but—"

"There'll always be a soft spot in my heart for all our creative people, Kevin. You know that. And especially our writers. But, as president, my principal responsibility has to be to the company, the income-producing mechanism on which literally hundreds of livelihoods—"

The check was brought on a silver tray, and the Dragon Lady signed it with her golden pen. Only when she was out of the country—say, in Paris or London—did she deign to pay for food and drink with her platinum American Express.

They rose from their table and made their way across the lavish dining room to the door. A snarling tiger, festooned with arrows, lay thrashing in its death throes on the muraled wall.

"The Shambler movie's all primed for a June release," burbled the Dragon Lady optimistically, as the massive bronze door of the Mumtaz Mahal swung open and they stepped out into the sunlit street. "I saw some of the rushes while I was out in California. They looked terrific. We're going to hold a special New York screening in January, Kevin. Better remind Naomi to reserve you a pair of tickets. I'd feel just wretched if you and Eugènie didn't get to see the final cut before the public did."

CHAPTER 17

▼

Kevin rose from the card table and smeared another Triscuit with Velveeta cheese. He scrounged a few half-melted ice cubes from the plastic bag and poured himself another styrofoam cupful of Coke. Fifteen feet away, rheumy-eyed comic artist Ed Scanlon, who lived in the neighborhood, hunched over the service counter nearest the cash register, conducting his habitual owl-like Saturday afternoon surveillance of the adolescents and preadolescents poring over the comics racks to ascertain which of them were electing to buy the comic books containing his work.

Kevin had agreed to do this signing months ago, well before the onset of his current financial crunch, but despite the fact that he would have much rather been elsewhere, he took it as a point of professional pride that he never knowingly disappointed a retailer or a fan. Not that he understood why Howie Bingham, jovial proprietor of Gotham Comics, would really want him in the first place, considering that he hadn't published any new stories in months.

Still, over the course of the last thirteen years, Kevin had scripted just about every title in the Dynamic line, and between the available back issues, and now the trade-paperback Shambler reprints, there was still a fairly impressive amount of material on hand for fans to buy and for him to sign. And of course some fans brought their own books with them from home, hermetically sealed against the ravages of acid and sunlight inside tightly fitting mylar bags. Inevitably, of course, there were also youngsters who hadn't the foggiest notion of who he was, and who consequently presented him with comic books to sign that he had not written, but Kevin always flashed them his most cordial smile and did his best to be extra nice to them.

In common with most comics shops, this one had been under-capitalized from its inception, and, amid the swiftly gentrifying environs of the Upper West Side, a bare half-mile walk from Kevin's brownstone, it stuck out as easily the scruffiest store on the block. Dingy T-shirts adorned with iron-on cartoons sagged limply from walls needy of spackling, together with faded posters extolling the virtues of comic books whose shelf lives had passed into extinction twelve months ago. The shops were the contemporary successors to pool halls—dismally drab, tawdry places where a barely pubescent young male clientele sought an outlet for its intense libidinous frustrations and yearnings through an obsession with gaudy, bright-colored geegaws in a frantic attempt to hold at bay their barely contained desperation for violence and sex. Indeed, standing there by the rickety card table that had been set up for the signing, eyeing the restless, vaguely discomfiting gaggle of socially maladroit males, Kevin felt certain he—

"Excuse me," inquired a pleasant-sounding female voice. "Are you Kevin Ellman?"

Kevin turned to find himself facing a woman in her mid-to-late thirties, slightly but not displeasingly overweight, with medium-length auburn hair, expansive brown eyes, an open, engaging smile, and a heavily pockmarked face.

"Yes, I'm Kevin Ellman," he answered. "But how—"

She gestured toward the hand-lettered placard in the shop's window proclaiming his appearance. "You were the only one in here who looked old enough to be"—and here she paused—"famous."

Kevin smiled benevolently.

"Are you famous?" she asked him ingenuously. "Should I really know who you are?"

Kevin shrugged amiably. "Only if you're into comic books," he replied.

"Kevin created the Shambler," chimed in Howie Bingham, earnestly endeavoring to do Kevin a good deed. "He's one of Dynamic's most important—"

"Dynamic is a comic book company," interjected Kevin, responding to the woman's bewildered look. "I write stories for them. That one on the counter is mine, and that—"

"I don't think I ever read comics," mused the woman, reflecting. "My parents always thought they—no, wait! I did read one! I—"

"*Archie,*" offered Kevin blandly.

"*Archie!* Yes! Are those the ones with Betty and—and—"

"Veronica."

"With Betty and Veronica?"

Kevin nodded.

"Yes! I did read those! But how did—"

Kevin allowed himself an indulgent little smile. It was the same smile his father had always given him after pulling a piece of candy out of Kevin's ear.

"I live just two, no three, blocks from here," she went on, pointing out through the shop's window and westward toward the river. "I pass by here every day on my way home from work, and I look in the window, but I don't think I've ever understood what really goes on in here. It looks so fascinating, you know. I mean, it looks as though everybody's really having a good time. But it also looks a little, you know, inhospitable in here or something—sort of like a cult, or maybe a shop where they fix motorcycles. Like if you don't really know what it's all about already, the people don't really want you to come in."

Poor Howie Bingham shot Kevin a definitely dismayed look, but Kevin found himself liking this girl immensely. He'd already begun, in fact, pondering the salutary effects of having her travel around the country to comic shops holding seminars on retailing.

"Oh, god! I haven't offended you guys or anything, have I?" she asked.

"Not in the least," reassured Kevin gently.

"So just now I passed by again, and I saw your poster, plus what seemed like sort of a little party going on, and I—"

"Can you tell us your name?" inquired Howie Bingham.

"Sure. Nan Wasserman," she replied.

"I'm Howie Bingham. I own this shop. Co-own it, really. I only wish—"

Kevin glanced at his watch. It was nearly 6:00 PM. "We're just about through for today, aren't we, Howie?"

"Oh, sure, Kev. God, you've really put in a long one, haven't you? I can't thank you enough for—"

Kevin reached down behind the card table and retrieved his Dynamic windbreaker, the spiffy blue satin one from last Christmas with his name, Kevin, stitched in yellow script above the front pocket and the company's crossed-lightning-bolts logo emblazoned on the back. In the zippered inside pocket, three rolls of quarters formed a lump as bulky and portentous as lead.

"Looks like we're losing our celebrity," remarked Nan brightly. "Getting set for a heavy Saturday-night date?"

"Uh-uh," answered Kevin with a quick shake of his head. "Just going to grab myself a quick bite to eat some—"

"There's a dynamite Chinese place on Broadway. Mind if I come along?"

CHAPTER 18

▼

"… with an ear punch, so that the left ear tells you its date of birth while the right one encodes its gender and whether it belongs to 'A' group, 'B' group, or Control."

Most of what she said had sailed way over Kevin's head, but he had begun to perk up considerably now that she had begun telling him about the rats. Nan Wasserman was a microbiologist like Anselm Parnell, the man who had become the Shambler, and she was evidently engaged in postdoctoral research at Columbia University having to do with hormones, or with one specific hormone in particular, but having precariously little to do with ordinary life.

"… only part I hate is having to sacrifice them," she explained ruefully.

"The rats?"

"Once they've been used in an experiment, you have to sacrifice them."

The beef with broccoli was good at this place. Kevin liked it.

"We do it with a little guillotine," she explained.

Kevin was incredulous. "You behead the rats?"

"It's the most painless way," she nodded gravely, "but you're right, it's still horrible. We keep it in a separate room so the rats in their cages can't hear the other rats squealing. I mean, they don't usually squeal when we actually, um, do it, but sometimes when you grab them and hold them they squeal, and this way the ones in the cages can't hear them. And also we're always careful, at least *I'm* always careful, to wipe off the blood after each one, so that when we bring another one in, he can't smell the—"

"Because?"

"It terrifies them. But in spite of what we do, no matter how careful, sometimes it hurts them and—and sometimes they know."

Kevin poured himself another cup of tea. He would have refilled her cup, too, but she still hadn't touched the first one he'd poured her.

"You hardly said a word until I started telling you about the rats."

"Some of it was a little hard to understand," Kevin admitted.

"It's hard to explain to someone who isn't in the field," she allowed half-apologetically. "But I hate just going out with other microbiologists."

"It was interesting," Kevin reassured her, "just a little difficult to understand."

"Is that all you do," she asked, "write comic books?"

Kevin nodded an enthusiastic yes.

"I didn't exactly mean that the way it sounded," she said apologetically. "I mean, um, you couldn't have gone to college to learn to write comic books, right?"

"Right," affirmed Kevin. "I probably would've majored in the humanities, in English, but I dropped out of college before—"

"To write comic books?"

Kevin nodded at her again, his eyes narrowing.

"Didn't your parents—"

"Look," interrupted Kevin, straining hard not to sound either argumentative or patronizing, "not everyone—"

"You're right. No, you're right," she stammered defensively. "It's just that—I don't think I've ever gone out with a man who didn't finish college before."

They finished their meal and Kevin called for the check, which arrived along with a pair of fortune cookies and a half-dozen orange slices. Kevin's fortune said, "You will marry your present lover and be happy." When Nan volunteered to pay her share, Kevin politely declined, but he waited till she'd risen from the table and turned toward the door before setting down two rolls of quarters and a meager handful of loose change.

"I'm sorry if I hurt your feelings in there," she said as the two of them stepped out onto the sidewalk

Kevin gave her a noncommittal shrug. "No problem," he said.

"Maybe next week sometime you'd like to see my lab."

CHAPTER 19

▼

The telephone was ringing when Kevin got home.

"Hey, Kevin, what's with all this scuttlebutt the little bird's been puttin' out about how you been sweatin' out some hard times lately, eh, pal?

"Gallante?"

"Us pros've gotta stick together, eh, pally, otherwise the friggin' companies're just gonna stick it to us one by one, right?"

"Look, Guido, dammit. Who the hell told—"

"Aw, c'mon, Kevin, you been around long enough to know what a fucking old whore this business is, right? It's like a fart—you know what I mean?—it just floats around on the wind. So I heard you was havin' some trouble, and I figured maybe I should call you up, see if—"

"You could help me out?"

"Right. You got it. 'Cause next time it'll prob'ly be me in trouble, and when—"

"What's your proposition, Guido?"

"Hunh-?!"

"Exactly what've—"

"Proposition? I ain't got no proposition, Kevin. It's just that I been killin' the bear pretty good this year—knock wood, right?—and I figure, well, if the shoe was on the other foot—"

Gallante's voice trailed off. Kevin paused reflectively. "Okay, you're right, Guido," he said finally. "I could use a loan—"

"Hey, Kev, great! That's just—"

"—but that doesn't mean I'm ready to get my kneecaps busted."

"Kneecaps whaat?! You been readin' too goddam many of your own funnybooks, you know that, Kevin? I'm in the same goddam racket as you, for chrissake—bustin' my nuts for page rate same as everybody else. And, yeah, I've bankrolled a few guys who've come up against it every now and again, and I even charged 'em a few points for my trouble. But you ain't never once heard of anyone gettin' hurt on account'a me, right? You know this business as well as I do, dammit. Anything like that—"

"Guido, look. I—"

"—went down, you'd tumble to it in a minute, right? So don't feed me this bullshit about kneecaps, Kevin. Just 'cause I work to better myself don't exactly qualify me as a king of crime."

"Guido, listen. I'm sorry. I never—"

"Look, I'm sorry, too. I lost it a little and I'm sorry. I mean, what's to argue about anyway, right? We're practically brothers. And you're broke, right? You're on the balls of your ass?"

Kevin whistled thinly as he sucked in his breath. "Yes," he confided quietly, "I am."

"Okay, fine, so let's not try and offend each other anymore. Let's just try and help each other. How much you need?"

"I'm not sure. I have—"

"Word is you tried and hit up on the Dragon Lady. How much was that?"

"I-I don't even remember," stammered Kevin, stunned that Gallante knew about it. "I hardly even—"

"Forget it, Kevin, look. It's just to tide you over the bumps till you retool your game, right? Till you get back to battin' out them scripts again, three, four—"

"Yes, I suppose—"

"Well, okay. So you don't need no major hunk of cash. What you need's a draw."

"Well, yes, I—"

"Just two or three grand a month or so to head off—"

"And the interest?"

"Damn it, Kevin, will you forget that? Just fuck the interest, okay? Just piss on it. Look, I'll tell you what. You'll get your draw, and if after three months you don't need it no more, piss on it, you just repay what I lent you and maybe I'm out a few beans I could've earned at the bank. But what the hell? So maybe you'll do me a favor someday. After three months, I know you, you'll be up to your asshole in some hot new series again. If not, so okay, then I'll probably have to start chargin' you some kinda interest. 'Cause that's only fair, right? Just please, for chrissake, don't help yourself to my generosity and then start hangin' out rumors on the vine about how I'm some kinda sleazy lowlife just 'cause I was out scufflin' for empties out in Bay Ridge while you was livin' high off the hog in Teaneck."

CHAPTER 20

▼

Skritch skritch! Skritch skritch! Rats in comic books made that sound as they scurried through sewage pipes or scrabbled frantically across mildewed cobblestone floors. But not these rats, all powder-puff pink and snowy white, whose gleaming multi-tiered steel-cage apartment complex all but touched the ceiling, its furry tenants clambering inquisitively along the barred walls or serenely gorging themselves on plentiful quantities of food and drink as they unwittingly awaited the next injection, the next dissection, the guillotine.

Nan was volubly endeavoring to explain the essence of her work to him, despite the fact that it was virtually all incomprehensible to Kevin, and, like most people engaged in a highly technical field of expertise, she displayed not the slightest inclination to modify her jargon so as to couch it in language he might understand. She was all pink and white, too, like the rats, enveloped in an oversized lab coat, only her head and limbs protruding, so that, except for her blue-and-white running shoes, it was impossible for him to tell how she was dressed—although she still had the auburn hair, of course, the engaging smile, the pockmarked face.

"Once the antidiuretic hormone vasopressin enters the excretory system, our research shows that it stimulates the—"

When Kevin was a little boy, once, at camp, one of the kids in his bunk had had a pet white rat, but their asshole of a counselor had forbidden him to keep that rat inside, so it was left in its cage outside, beneath the cabin floor, with a towel folded up beside it to keep it warm. They'd found it the following morning—frozen to death, and blue—and held a funeral for it in a lashing rain. Kevin could still recall standing there in his yellow slicker, with his head bowed and the rain streaming down, as the rat was laid to its final rest in a dilapidated Muriel cigar box ("Why don't you come up and … smoke me sometime?") along with an offering of chocolates, a few marbles, and a handful of coins.

After a while, Nan gave up trying to make him understand the hormone experiments and together they exited Schermerhorn and cut across the quadrangle to the subway entrance on Broadway and a Hundred-and-sixteenth. Even at this hour there were cute girls everywhere, and Kevin permitted himself to become distracted by imagining a few of them in stockings and garter belts.

They ate dinner at a good Mexican restaurant in Kevin's neighborhood, then strolled down Columbus Avenue for awhile before turning east on Seventy-first Street a half-block to the brownstone where Kevin lived. Drug addicts and homeless men, formerly in the habit of picking through neighborhood garbage cans in search of returnable bottles and cans, had lately taken to overturning the garbage cans completely, strewing their contents everywhere, with the result that the tiny stairwell just outside the basement-level entranceway to Kevin's apartment was now routinely transformed into a miniature dump.

Apologizing profusely for the reeking, ungodly mess, Kevin trailblazed a path through the garbage pile and ushered his companion inside. The Cat's Paw clock gleamed grotesquely, like some baleful eye, and the New Guinea spirit mask actually seemed to glower, as though renouncing, through its own volition, its primal protective role.

"Oh my god!" Nan gasped.

"It's from New Guinea," explained Kevin, switching on the pole lamp, transforming the darkened room into a mottled patchwork of dark and light. "It's protecting us against evil spirits."

"You were in New Guinea?" she exclaimed.

"I only pray I never live so long," laughed Kevin. "I sublet this place from an anthropologist. He's there now. But—"

"But?"

"—but if he gets eaten, I could probably get the lease."

She laughed then, which was nice, and she hadn't criticized the unholy mess the place was in, which was nice, too.

"You have an awful lot of tapes," she called out to him, as he withdrew to the kitchen to put on some water for the instant coffee.

"Right," he answered. "I—"

"Who's—who's Angel Hart?"

"Stripper, porn star," replied Kevin.

She appeared in the entranceway to the kitchen with a videocassette in each hand. "These are all porno tapes?" she asked him.

"Those two are," he answered her matter-of-factly, glancing at her over his shoulder as he spooned the freeze-dried into a pair of mugs. "But you'll also—"

"You're really into it?"

"Porn?"

"Uh-huh."

"Sure, sometimes," he admitted.

The water on the stove was boiling now, and Kevin lifted off the kettle with an oven mitt and poured the water into the mugs, watching as it welled up toward the rim like sludge.

"Milk?" he asked her.

She shook her head. "It's not that I'm judgmental about it. I think people should be allowed to fantasize."

"Sugar?" inquired Kevin.

She shook her head again. "Don't you agree?"

"What? That people should be allowed to fantasize?"

"Yes."

"Of course I do," answered Kevin.

"I guess you'd pretty much have to," she laughed. "If it weren't for fantasy, you'd be out of business."

They returned to the living room, and Kevin preempted the armchair, leaving her to take the couch. Ever since he'd gone out on his first date, years ago, deciphering those subtle sexual signals women were reputed to send had seemed a well-nigh-impossible task to Kevin, and it was out of his despair of ever being able to divine those particular sorts of entrails properly that he had developed his own patented seductive technique. Typically, Kevin would invite a girl to his apartment and sit down and talk with her for hours, never once making a provocative or untoward overture of any kind. If, by the time it got to be around 3:00 AM, she still hadn't made a move to leave, then, and only then, would he sit down beside her and perhaps even take her hand. And then he'd wait, because it was an absolutely ironclad rule with him that the next move had to be hers. Kevin knew full well that his *modus operandi* was highly idiosyncratic, but he also knew that it served to circumvent the agony of rejection almost completely, and, in any event, that it had never failed to work for him.

Kevin and Nan chatted on for hours, and ultimately, at the appointed time, after returning from the kitchen with the umpteenth round of coffee, Kevin bypassed the armchair and sat down a discreet distance away from her on the couch. They talked a lot about comic books, which was a good thing, Kevin thought, because that hormone stuff she did with rats was really boring—at least it was really boring the way *she* talked about it—and within fifteen minutes she had reached out and gently taken his hand in hers. She even started stroking his fingers with her thumb, which was an extremely positive sign, and, clasping her hand in his, Kevin could feel she had begun to sweat.

Kevin got up and made them another cup of coffee, and this time, after he'd returned from the kitchen and sat down even closer to her, she placed her hand gently on the back of his neck and turned his head slightly toward her and kissed him tenderly, passionately, on the mouth. This kiss was long and wet and good, and Kevin felt fairly confident now that she was ready to do it with him—but only after they'd kissed twice more, and she'd reached up to unbutton the top two or three buttons of her blouse, was Kevin certain that it was completely safe. He undid the remaining buttons for her, the bottom ones first, then unhooked her brassiere and put his mouth to her breasts. She ran her hands through his hair, exhibiting not the slightest inclination to resist him, and so he stood up from the sofa, taking her gently by the hand, and led her into his tiny bedroom, large enough to accommodate only a double bed, a modest bookcase, and a small chest of drawers. Even so, the floor was littered with comic books and old *TV Guides*, making it difficult for any but an initiate to avoid tripping and falling in the semidarkness.

Kevin lighted an oversized candle that he kept in an aluminum-foil-lined saucer atop the dresser and cast a sidelong glance at her as they undressed in the flickering light. The surge of excitement and self-confidence he'd felt while kissing her was waning, and Kevin suddenly began to panic that it might vanish completely. He tried to convince himself that it was because she was not beautiful, but deep down he knew that this nearly always happened the moment he was actually on the verge of having sex with them. It was a lot like writing, only much worse than writing, because for all the nerve-wracking demands it made, at least writing was solitary and humiliation infrequent. Nonetheless, with lovemaking as with plotting stories, all you could do was try to relax, and let your mind go free, and pray that the magic came to you when you needed it, like a gift.

They lay side by side on the bed now, with Kevin kissing her softly, fondling her breasts and thighs, and struggling to maintain control of his breathing, to keep it measured and regular, to perpetuate, as it were, the illusion that he was engaged in a strategy of patient, deliberate foreplay and not a desperate effort to keep a rising tide of terror from drowning his ability to perform.

The heady arousal that had taken hold of him in the living room had ebbed completely now, or nearly so, but she had begun gently stroking his cock with her hand, and that was good. It firmed and stiffened as she stroked it, and while the anxiety still fluttered through him like moths on a night wind, his breathing was even and unlabored and he no longer feared at any instant he might start gasping for air.

Then she slid down toward the foot of the bed and began to suck him, her moist lips enveloping the head of his cock and then inching their way up the shank like snails. Octavia had been afflicted with genital herpes, and all at once Kevin became fearful that he might have unwittingly contracted it from her and was now passing it along to Nan through her mouth. He fantasized that he had somehow acquired AIDS without knowing it and was now inflicting a slow-acting death with his cock.

And yet somehow these fantastic anxieties had the effect of dissolving his more realistic ones. An awesome, tremulous excitement surged through him, electrifying his body from head to toe. He knotted his hand in her hair and began to moan.

Good god! He was going to come! He hardly knew this girl, and yet here he was about to fill her mouth with come! He frantically flashed on Eugènie's frogs, on the Shambler grubbing for maggots amid the Himalayan drifts, on invisible microorganisms multiplying beneath the toilet seat and crawling unimpeded into his rectum. It helped a little, but not completely. The overwhelming arousal was far too strong. He wrenched his cock free of her lips and slid down beside her, guiding his impatient erection between the oozing lips of her cunt. It was far from perfect but at least it was not a disaster. He managed two or three strong strokes before he finally came.

"I'm sorry," he whispered.

"Shh," she replied. "Don't be silly."

Kevin blew out the candle and lay down beside her. Within moments the two of them were sound asleep.

It was the inhuman jangle of the telephone that jolted him awake.

"Kevin?"

"Who…?" stammered Kevin uncomprehendingly.

"It's me. Hinder. Jesus Christ, Kev! Don't tell me you're still—"

The clock radio on the dresser glowed 2:10 PM. And Nan was gone. Her clothes—

"And here I thought you were always up and about by the crack of noon."

—were gone, too. But her wristwatch—

"That was a dumb maneuver, Kevin. Dumb."

"What?!"

"You know what I mean. Going to lunch with the Dragon Lady. What'd you do, ask her for money?"

—her wristwatch still lay atop the dresser, where she'd put it when they got undressed. To Kevin, it was a sure sign that she—

"Kevin? You there?"

"Uh-huh."

"Did you ask her for money?"

"The Dragon Lady?"

"Yes, of course the Dragon Lady."

"Yes, I asked her for—"

"I told you I'd lend you money if you needed it, Kevin."

And here Hinder paused, but Kevin said nothing.

"Don't you remember I told you that?"

"Why shouldn't I have asked her for money, Ron?" exclaimed Kevin, exasperated. "She's the company, for christ's sake. They've—"

"Because it's a sign of weakness, Kev—like starting to tremble all over when you suddenly find yourself face to face with a Kodiak bear. They can smell—"

"I don't give a shit, Ron."

"Kevin. For Pete's sake. She's taken you off the Cicada. No warning, no nothing. Just bounced it over to Davidoff—just like that. Kevin, I don't know what the hell you did, but you—"

"I don't give a fuck, Ron."

"Kev?"

"I don't give a fuck about the Dragon Lady and I don't give a fuck about the Silver Cicada. The creativity's within *me,* Ron, not in the Cicada and not in any other damn character. So when I'm good and ready, I'll do something else, Ron. And in the meantime—"

"Kev? Kev, I—"

"—why don't you tell the Dragon Lady she can just go fuck herself!"

CHAPTER 21

▼

"I'm Greg, paleobotany," volunteered the young man pleasantly. "What's your field?"

"Comics," answered Kevin. "I'm in the comics field."

"Kevin writes comic book stories," interjected Nan, by way of explanation.

They were in a large apartment on West End Avenue teeming with graduate students and younger members of the Columbia faculty. The rooms were sparsely furnished, and framed pictures and other decorative flourishes were rare. Scholarly books and journals packed the makeshift wall-length bookcases haphazardly fashioned from scavenged lengths of old lumber and bricks. The guests milled about the apartment in close-knit groups, heatedly embroiled in academic gossiping and theoretical disputes. Both males and females were amply represented, but no one seemed very much interested in sex.

"Mihri! Come here a minute! Nan's friend—"

"Kevin."

"Kevin. Sorry. Mihri, Kevin writes comic books."

"It's nice to meet you Kevin. I'm Mihri. But, Greg, I don't think I know what they are, comic—"

"Oh, for heaven's sake, Mihri. Of course you do. Comic books are—"

The girl, Mihri, was short, about five-foot-two, with olive skin and thick, nearly shoulder length, dark brown hair. She was not beautiful—she had obese thighs, for one thing, and there was an air about her that was vaguely intimidating—but she had huge soft brown eyes that Kevin liked a lot and, notwithstanding her unfashionably loose-fitting clothing, Kevin could see that she had pendulous breasts.

"… Greg," she was saying, "I don't even know if we *have* them in Turkey, and if we do—"

"You draw them, too, is that right, Kevin?" inquired Greg, who had an affable smile and steel-rimmed eyeglasses and curly blond hair.

"No, I just write them," clarified Kevin. "Somebody else—"

"You mean somebody actually writes those things?" chimed in the voice of another guest, new to the conversation. "I never knew somebody actually wrote them!"

The newcomer, who wore a gold I.D. bracelet identifying her as Nadia, was clad in an ankle-length black skirt and a cracked leather World War II bomber jacket covered with Air Force patches—surmounted by a delicately high-cheekboned face and a shock of blond hair carefully coiffed into a style of sensual disarray.

"You mean you're the one who makes up the words that go inside those little bubbles?" she persisted.

"Balloons," corrected Kevin gently.

"Balloons. Sorry."

"And the words that go along the tops of the frames, too, right?" asked Greg.

"The frames are called panels," explained Kevin.

"Oh, god, I remember they were so fabulous!" Greg went on. "I read a million of them when I was a kid. No kidding, I bet I'd accumulated over two thousand of them before—"

"Your mother pitched them out," interjected Nadia.

"Oh no, nothing like that. It's just that I went to college, and my kid brother got them, and god only—"

"I think it may be we did have them in Turkey," mused Mihri, "but I'm sure I never—"

"My all-time favorite was Power Man," recalled Greg wistfully. "Is he still—"

"He's still published," affirmed Kevin, "but I'm afraid he's not nearly as popular as he used to be. In fact, if it weren't for—"

"And how about the Black Bat? He was incredible, wasn't he?"

"He still is," replied Kevin. "And he seems to be—"

"How'd you two guys meet, anyway?" interrupted Nadia, a bit impatiently.

"At one of Kevin's signings," replied Nan.

"Signing?" Mihri asked.

"At a comic shop," explained Kevin. "We make guest appearances at them in order to—"

"Kevin created the Shambler," broke in Nan proudly.

"Shambler," murmured Greg reflectively. "Hmm. I can't say as—"

"They're even making a Shambler movie," exclaimed Nan.

"Movie? How wonderful!" cried Mihri. "We'll all have to go see it as soon as it comes out!"

Kevin and Nan left the party a short while later and strolled down Broadway to catch the Eighty-sixth Street crosstown bus. Kevin spied the Gotham Video Shop the moment they got off, a few blocks from her apartment house on the Upper East Side.

"Got a VCR?" inquired Kevin suddenly.

"At my place? Sure. Why?"

"I was thinking it might be fun if we rented a tape."

The place was packed, teeming with the hustle and bustle of the home-bound Friday night crowd. Effortlessly eluding Nan in the crush, Kevin fought his way to the rear, where they kept the shelves of X-rated tapes. His first biweekly check from Guido Gallante, all fifteen hundred dollars of it, still reposed serenely in his pocket, uncashed, but he knew he'd brought enough cash with him to enable him to make the deposit and rent the tape. Nan caught up with him just as the checkout girl was peeling off the magnetized alarm strip and handing Kevin his receipt.

"Bimini Sluts?" she exclaimed incredulously.

Her entire apartment was carpeted, and everywhere Kevin looked it was clear that stringent measures were in effect to prevent any buildup of dust. Nan had slipped off into her tiny kitchen to fix them some tea, leaving Kevin to pull off his shoes and tiptoe tentatively around the dismayingly tidy living room looking for a place an ordinary, presumably germ-laden, human being might be allowed to sit down. A clutch of plexiglass-box picture frames clustered together on one wall housed Kodacolor snapshots of Nan gamely rafting through foaming rapids with a trio of other girls, romping in what looked like a hayfield with an English sheepdog and two young children, and as the maid of honor at the suburban wedding of a bride with the steel-sinewed delicacy of a ballerina and a huge, scowling bear of a man with an unkempt red beard. On the wall opposite was a large work of art, evidently meant to be taken seriously, in the form of a collage of geometrically shaped pieces of multicolored felt intricately linked together with lengths of gold and silver string.

A teakwood cabinet housed the television. Kevin switched it on and inserted *Sluts* into the VCR. Whichever asshole had rented the tape previously hadn't bothered to rewind it, thus compelling Kevin to perform the mildly irritating chore for him. Then the soothingly familiar images began to dance across the screen, grainy at first, and marred by aggravating little jumps or cuts, which made Kevin grit his teeth with annoyance at having gotten stuck with an inferior print.

Across the room from the television was an armchair, and although it looked forbiddingly pristine, Kevin finally decided to chance it. Like the ottoman directly in front of it, and the expanse of plush carpet surrounding it, it was a brownish-white, sandy color, and yet it also had undertones of salmon in it, or coral, like the reflection of a sunset on a Caribbean beach. In an odd way, it was reminiscent of those red-sandstone buttes out in New Mexico, where Jordan Mason lived.

"Kevin?"

"Huh-!? Oh god! I am allowed to sit here, aren't I?"

"Don't be silly. Of course."

"Almost finished with the tea?"

"In a minute. The water's—"

"Good. Come here, then. Quick. There's a good spot coming. We're coming to the spot where they do threesies with the old social director who's dressed up as a pirate."

"How do you know that?"

"Huh-?!"

"Have you seen this film before?"

"Sure. I—"

"You mean you rented this film and—and you've already seen it?"

"Nan, everybody rents films they've—"

"Kevin?"

"Damn it, it's already started. Hold on a minute. I'll get up and re—"

"Kevin, it's late."

"What?"

"It's late. And I don't feel right. And I have to go to the lab tomorrow. There's this—"

"Tomorrow? Saturday?"

"—experiment and I—"

"Tomorrow?"

"I just feel shitty, Kevin. Something I ate, maybe, at the—"

"You want me to go?"

She averted her face slightly and nodded, casting her large brown eyes at the floor.

Kevin seated himself astride the ottoman and pulled on his shoes. "Think you could return the movie for me?" he asked her. "I've already—"

"Sure, why not?"

CHAPTER 22

▼

The old steel-rimmed eyeglass frames pinched Kevin's nose, and his beard and mustache itched, but Kevin felt these simple precautions were more than justified, and he felt both relieved and vindicated when the cashier failed to recognize him—even though it was not the same cashier who had participated in ejecting him the last time he was here. Hovering anxiously about the jam-packed rotunda until he saw Vicki's booth was clear, he scurried inside, threw the door latch, noting that it had been completely replaced since his last visit, and dropped his tokens—chug-chug—into the slot.

The booth lights blinked out like moribund stars. The black panel began to rise. Amid the burgeoning corona of light seeping steadily outward from the adjoining booth where his lovely Vicki awaited him, Kevin could make out the glossy, slightly mismatched areas of Spackle and fresh paint that marked the places where his conduct during his previous visit had compelled the management to effect repairs.

"Hi, there!" chirped a slightly weary but determinedly cheerful voice. "I'm—"

"Oh, god! Vicki!" exclaimed Kevin ecstatically. "It's—"

He cut himself off abruptly in mid-sentence, struck dumb by her confounded look. And then all at once he remembered the beard and mustache and frantically began to tear them off. "Vicki, it's me!" he cried. "Kev—"

But the excess spirit gum he'd applied had congealed into an adhesive, gummy mess and the recalcitrant disguise would not relinquish its terrible hold on his face. Kevin hadn't worn the damn thing since the Costume-Con for World Hunger, in Minneapolis, where he'd appeared in a skit as one of the Galaxy Guardians, and he'd long since lost track of the bottle of special stuff you were supposed to use to—

"Kevin? Omigod! Is that—"

Kevin grabbed a loose corner of beard in his fingers, clenched his lower lip courageously, and wrenched the hairy morass free. The mustache surrendered meekly after only a token struggle. Kevin stood there with a sheepish look on his face, panting—

"Kevin?"

—waiting for the painful stinging to go away.

"Kevin, what the fuck—"

And then her eyes locked onto his and she started to laugh. Kevin wasn't at all sure whether he was supposed to laugh with her, but the sparkle in her eye was so infectious that he just couldn't help himself. So now they were both laughing, and Kevin was feeling so blissfully happy he didn't think he'd ever be able to stop.

It had to be Vicki who sobered up first. "Kevin, why on earth—"

"Last time I was here," stammered Kevin, "—they said if I came back—"

"Kevin, you are an effing maniac! Are your comic books—"

"Vicki, I love you!" blurted Kevin.

"Kevin, look—"

"I know how it sounds. I know it probably sounds—"

"Kevin—"

"—but, crazy or not, it's true. And I wouldn't have come back after the last time, ever, if—"

"Kevin, baby—"

"I just want you to go out with me. To try it just once. I just want—"

"Kevin, baby, look. You seem like a really special guy to me, you know what I mean? I mean, a zillion guys ask me to go out around here, okay, but you—"

"Okay, then, we—"

"But I just can't do it, Kev. It's okay if I call you Kev, right? I'd lose my job Kevin. My bosses—"

"But why would they ever—"

"They just would, Kevin. I'd lose my goddam job. I mean, it may not be the world's most fabulous job, you know what I mean? But—"

"Then what am *I* supposed to do?" cried Kevin plaintively. "How—"

"You've just gotta keep comin' back to see me here, Kev, in the booth. That's just what you've gotta do. I know it's not cheap, but we can see each other a lot this way, I promise. And you don't havta wear that disguise anymore, I mean it. I'll even go speak to my boss about it if I have to, okay? I'll have him tell those gorillas not to hassle you no more, okay? But you can't go out of control no more, right?"

Her lips were a luscious, liquid crimson.

"You gotta promise me to be good from now on—"

Her eyes shone like polished tourmaline. Kevin was afraid he was going to swoon dead away.

"—okay?"

CHAPTER 23

▼

"… glad to get back to you just as soon as I can."

Beeep!

"Hello, Kevin? It's me, Nan. I tried to call you a few times … two times, anyway, but I guess you were … it's just that I don't want to seem … Kevin? I-I mean I don't think we should go out anymore. I mean I think you're a wonderful guy, Kevin. A lovely, lovely guy. But I just don't think we're compatible, you know what I mean? I just think maybe we aren't, okay…?"

Kevin thought fleetingly about taking her call, then decided against it, figuring what the hell would be the point? He finished zipping up his down winter coat and double-locked the front door, then stepped outside into a light, steady snowfall to catch a bus down Central Park West to Forty-ninth Street and Broadway and trudge the four long crosstown blocks east to Dynamic Comics. The avenues were all but gridlocked with holiday shoppers, a poignant reminder to Kevin that with Dynamic's yuletide blowout barely ten days away, all signs pointed toward his going alone. Eugènie had always attended the party with him and had always hated it—and for the same reason that she had always hated every gathering of comics folk—because all anyone ever did at them was stand around talking about comic books. What made the Christmas party even worse, she complained, was that the people had to *scream* about comic books because they played the music so loud you couldn't even hear yourself think. "At a company headed by a seventy-year-old woman," she griped, "you'd think the policy would be to keep the volume down!"

Arriving at Dynamic's twelfth-floor reception area, Kevin found the massive bronze statue of Power Man already festively bedizened in a bright-red velour Santa cap and a matching shoulder sack brimful of colorfully beribboned, gaily wrapped gifts—a holiday image of the superhero as a super-giver of gifts that had been discomfitingly desecrated, in Kevin's view, by the wholly unauthorized, anonymous addition to the statue of a pair of pointy elfin ears. It wasn't that Kevin lacked a sense of humor; he merely felt that a modicum of respect was in order for the hand, bronze or otherwise, responsible for feeding you your daily bread.

His ostensible reason for coming here today was to pick up his complimentary monthly bundle of comic books, but even Kevin knew that was only a pretext. It was the second Friday of the month, freelancers were pouring in from throughout the metropolitan area to collect their paychecks, and now they lounged around the halls and offices, buttonholing editors, flirting with the pasteup girls, talking shop. Kevin may not have been doing any writing these days, but he still wanted to feel he had a hand in the game.

Sol Bernstein was there, beaming proudly as he held aloft the most recent additions to his Vera Hale collection—a pristine-mint queen of hearts and five of spades from a deck of early-nineteen-forties S & M playing cards—and regaled everyone within earshot with the tales of his latest attempts to unravel her whereabouts. Someone laughed and said if Bernstein ever did find her, he'd have nothing else to live for and would probably have to commit suicide, but someone else chimed in no, Bernstein would just have to find himself another project, like, say, tracking down Hale's great-great-grandmother, who, for all anyone knew, *might* have been a pinup queen during the Crimean War.

Kevin made his way down the long hallway, shaking hands with freelance friends and acquaintances, exchanging industry gossip and anecdotes, assuring them he'd be at the big holiday bash the week after next. He didn't especially relish the idea of running into the Dragon Lady while he was up here, but he knew that the chances of her abandoning the seclusion of her office for a stroll down the hallway at any time, let alone on a payday Friday, were remote. Feeling thirsty all of a sudden, he took a detour off the hallway into the diminutive company "kitchen," a tiny pantry-sized room equipped with a Pullman-sized refrigerator and ice maker, a coffee machine, and metal cabinets provisioned with free cans of Coke.

"Say! Kevin!" Pass me that fuckin' Cremora, willya, pal?"

"Sure," answered Kevin, snatching up the Cremora jar and sliding it down the formica counter. "How're things, Guido?"

"Me? Never better, guy. Never better. You know that new young editor they got here? The bimbo? With the zits? You know what?—she don't know pencil artwork from her asshole! I been crankin' out jobs for that little skirt so fast it's even makin' *my* head spin. Fastest bucks I—"

"What happens when she learns?"

"Learns what? That I'm givin' her shit? Who cares? By that time, I'll be sellin' to somebody else."

"Sucker born every minute, right?"

"At least. But enough about my life. How's the old writer's block comin'?"

Kevin winced.

"You worked out a way yet to—"

"Not yet," stammered Kevin nervously, clearing his throat. "But it's coming. It'll—"

"Hey, yeah, sure, Kevin!" proclaimed Gallante expansively. "It'll shake itself out, Kevin. I know that." Aided by a pair of peppermint-striped plastic stirrers, Gallante was manfully endeavoring to dissolve an obstinate clot of Cremora into the steaming, freshly poured contents of a styrofoam cup. "Scoring any pussy these days, Kevin?" he asked.

"Huh-?!"

"Pussy, Kevin," repeated Gallante, impatiently withdrawing the soggy Cremora-glopped stirrers from his coffee cup and disdainfully tossing them into a plastic-lined trash can. "What the hell's the matter with you? You don't understand me when I say 'pussy'?"

Kevin shrugged.

"That means no, right?" persisted Gallante. "No, you're not scoring any pussy?"

Kevin shrugged again. "I was seeing a girl," he answered quietly, "but—"

"I don't mean to tell you your business, Kevin, but you can't expect to write stories if you're not getting your tubes cleaned."

Kevin smiled wanly. "I have a friend in New Mexico who—"

"What? A woman?"

"No," replied Kevin, "a male friend. But he says the same—"

"Good. Then you got a smart friend." Gallante paused. "You want me to get you—"

"A woman?"

"Right."

"For money?" asked Kevin.

"No, for free."

"Free?"

"You keep on like this, you're gonna get me pissed off, Kevin."

"Pissed—"

"Because here I am floatin' you three G's a month interest free, and I hadda practically break your arm to get you to take it. Now I ask you if you want me to score you a bimbo, and all I'm hearin' is please can I look the gift horse in the mouth, in the ears, up the asshole. Am I getting through to you at all, Kevin?"

"Yes, Guido. And you're right. I'm sorry. But—"

"What?"

"I would like a woman. The problem is there's a specif—"

"Who?"

"*Who?*"

"Yeah, who? Here you're pining over some skirt you want but you can't get, so I'm—"

"But what difference does it make?" blurted Kevin.

"You're a difficult person to have an ordinary conversation with, you know that, Kevin?" scowled Gallante, shaking his head in mild exasperation.

"I met her in a one-on-one booth at the Pornomart. She—"

"Exactly what the fuck are we talkin' about here, Kevin—a cunt you jerked off in front of in some fuckin' peep show?"

"It's not a peep show, Guido. You—"

"You put in a quarter, right? Like a wall comes up?"

"Yes," Kevin nodded, "that—"

"And what's the place called? The—"

"The Pornomart."

"Near the bus station?"

Kevin nodded again. "Her name's—"

"What?"

"Vicki."

"Is she a blonde? Redhead? Bru—"

"Blond. With blue eyes. No, blue-green. And she—"

"You wouldn't settle for another blonde with blue-green eyes, wouldja, Kevin? Or maybe one with just regular old-fashioned blue eyes?"

"All cats are gray in the dark, right Guido?" exclaimed Kevin, sounding a good deal more sardonic than he'd intended.

Gallante had the oddest bemused look on his face. "Kevin of—"

"Guido, listen," interjected Kevin quickly, anxious to make amends. "I appreciate the generous thought, and I didn't mean to sound suspicious. I'm sorry."

"Hey, don't even mention it, pal," retorted Gallante, brightening. "And here's hoping old St. Nick puts something pink an' juicy in your stocking, eh, guy?"

CHAPTER 24

▼

The Stutz Bearcat was solid pewter, and fit neatly in the palm of the pretty model's hand. Each classic car in the series was a fifty-five-dollar value, but Shop-At-Home Cable was making them available for the first time in history for the unbelievable TV-giveaway price of only eighteen seventy-five.

Kevin was sorely tempted. There was something ineffably precious and rare about them, and, assembled together as a group, the ten cars looked absolutely stunning on their genuine walnut-veneer stand. Then, suddenly, the lot number on the screen changed from gold to red and began flashing on and off, the signal to the viewing audience that it had only half a minute left to make up its mind.

Kevin had never cared for cars particularly, and even when he was a boy, models, generally, had never held much interest for him. But these cars seemed somehow timeless and—and historic—

Twenty-eight seconds ... twenty-seven seconds ...

—there was no denying the price was a spectacular bargain—

... twenty-four seconds ...

—and Kevin never really knew when he might need to give a friend or acquaintance some sort of—

... twenty-two seconds ...

—gift. Of course, when you really thought about it, scale-model antique cars weren't really the sort of—

... nineteen ...

—thing you customarily bought for someone else. It was—

... eighteen ...

But still—

In another few moments, the ten-second buzzer would sound its warning and the toll-free number would start to flash. Once that happened, Kevin knew, it would be all but impossible for him to get his call through.

... seventeen ... sixteen ...

Kevin reached tentatively toward the telephone.

The buzzer exploded in his ear, louder—much louder—than he had ever heard it.

... fifteen ...

And too soon.

... fourteen ...

It exploded again. Twice this time, raucous and insistent.

... thirteen ... twel—

Good christ—it was the doorbell! Kevin sprang off the couch. The front doorbell! Some demented asshole was leaning on the doorbell at—at fucking 1:00 AM!

The intercom connecting his apartment with the outer gate had been moribund for decades, one of the quaintly rustic charms of brownstone life, leaving Kevin scant alternative but to fly down the hall to confront the night-stalking maniac face to face. Residing on the basement level, Kevin had all but resigned himself to the annoyance of having his routine periodically interrupted by nuisance callers of all kinds—from apartment seekers to exterminators to UPS deliverymen—all of whom assumed he must be the super, when, in fact, there was no super, and invariably leaned on his doorbell as though the building were burning down around him just when he was napping or trying to work. But all those intrusions occurred in the daytime. No one—

Kevin stared through the latticework of the wrought-iron gate and literally could not believe his eyes. All he could think of was that he must be seeing things, visions, on the order of a vividly imagined encounter with extraterrestrials or a miraculous visitation from the risen Christ. He blinked hard, squeezing the—

"Kevin Ellman lives here, right?" she asked him.

Kevin unlocked the gate and let her in. It was like dreaming of hippos, and his movements were dream movements, like the way he'd moved in the hippo dream.

It was the only dream of his childhood that he still remembered, the only dream whose images had remained with him, lucid, limpid, throughout all the years of his adult life. In it, he'd awakened one morning to find the entire house filled with water, flooded with water from the floors to the ceilings, and although he'd felt panicky at first, frightened of drowning, he soon discovered that he could breathe the water, that he could move in it and propel himself through it as effortlessly and gracefully as a dolphin or a seal. Swimming alongside him were hippopotamuses, huge, smooth behemoths whose ponderously graceful movements underwater exuded feelings of reassurance, warmth, protectiveness. Kevin swam among them, knowing that he was safe with them and always would be. His sister had not been born yet, and his parents, for some inexplicable dream reason, were absent from the house. And yet their absence was in no way alarming, as if the hippos—

"Oh Jesus! Shit!" he heard her exclaim. "I-I know you—from the booth!"

Kevin blinked again and looked at her.

"I know you from the booth!" she exclaimed again, her eyes flying like panicked starlings to the scrap of yellow paper she held clutched in one hand. "You're Kevin! I-I mean I knew you were Kevin, but I didn't know you were *that* Kevin! You're—"

Kevin gaped at her dumbly, like a poleaxed cow.

"—the comic book guy Kevin, right?"

Kevin nodded at her, as a drowned man might nod. He tried hard to say her name, but the name would not come out. "I don't understand," he stammered incoherently. "You're—"

"I never knew you knew Paul! How come you never said you knew Paul?"

"Paul?" echoed Kevin bewilderedly.

"Paul Haraldson!" She made it sound like an accusation. "You must—"

"It's freezing," commented Kevin quietly. "I'm freezing. Could we maybe discuss—"

"Discuss! Ha!" she proclaimed scornfully, sweeping past him down the hallway and then whirling round to face him at his apartment door as he scrambled to catch up with her. "I mean this is really weird, Kevin, you know that! You know what I mean, *weird?*"

"No, not really," answered Kevin distractedly, sidling past her into the apartment and hastily shoveling a few overturned stacks of comic books out of her way.

"Jesus! Shit!" She entered on tentative tiptoe behind him. "You don't know what I mean when I say *weird?*"

"No," replied Kevin again, shaking his head.

"What I mean is, I do this sometimes as a favor, Kevin, okay? But it's never guys from the booth, you know what I mean?" She glanced at the yellow scrap of paper again. "You're sure you're not one of Paul's—"

"No," Kevin assured her, but his mind's eye flashed abruptly on Guido Gallante.

"Okay, then I don't get it," she shrugged bewilderedly, unbuttoning her white-fur-trimmed fuchsia cloth winter coat and tossing it casually onto a chair, "but I guess—SHIT! THAT THING!"

"What thing?" Kevin asked her.

"That thing!"

"Oh, it's a spirit mask," he reassured her. "From New Guinea. It protects—"

"Shit! You mean like—like voodoo?!"

"I don't think so," answered Kevin. "The guy who—"

"Because I know you know me from the booth, Kevin, and I don't know what you're into, or what kind of bimbo you think I am or what I'm into. But I'm telling you right—"

"You don't know how wonderful it is to see you, Vicki," beamed Kevin. "I've dreamed—"

"But you're not into any really weird shit or anything, right, Kevin?"

"No, I don't think so," he replied.

"Because I don't mean costumes or anything like that," she went on. "I mean—"

She was wearing skintight emerald-green satin pants and a matching rhinestone-buttoned blouse, and in her black patent-leather shoes with four-inch-high translucent plexiglass spike heels, she was very nearly as tall as he was. She was stepping toward him now, unfastening the topmost button of her blouse, then the one beneath it.

"—how could I really know what you're into, right? If you like garters, in my purse.…"

She took his face in her hands and she kissed him, her satin sleeves rustling against him like sheets of cellophane in a wind. It was like a dream having her there alone with him, touching him, far from the booth. She kissed him again, sliding one hand deftly away from him this time, undoing the remaining buttons on her blouse, so that the virid garment fell open, revealing a lacy black brassiere with cutout holes for her nipples to show through.

Kevin harbored few illusions about just where his sexual proclivities lay. His apartment was piled high with pornography, and an inordinate proportion of his mental life was given over to lurid fantasies of every kind about carnal encounters with whores and sluts. But for whatever reasons one might care to attribute it to, Kevin had fallen in love with Vicki. He loved her. And he wanted her—but not for a one-night stand as his slut.

"Kevin?"

An uncanny chill fluttered through him like a moth aloft inside his body on a pair of ice wings.

"Kevin? Is something wrong?"

"No, why?"

"You want to fuck me, right, Kevin? I mean, in the booth—"

"Do you know Guido Gallante, Vicki?"

"Who?"

"Guido—"

"Gwee-doh? What the hell kind of faggot name is that?"

"Do you know him?"

"Fuck you, Kevin! You already asked me that and I told you no!"

"I'm sorry, Vicki. It's just—"

"I said I don't know him and that means I don't know him! I mean, why the hell should I lie to you?"

"I didn't think you lied. I just—"

"Just what?"

"Just—"

"This isn't some kind of crazy comic book bullshit, is it, Kevin? I mean, I came over here because Paul said I'd probably like you and I thought we could make it. When you were in the booth that time, you said you wanted to fuck me, remember? Only now—"

"In the booth that time, I said—"

"Okay, what?"

"—I loved you. I said—"

"Kevin! That's crazy!"

"—I wanted you to go out with me, on a date—"

"A date?!?"

"—outside the booth. I said I just wanted you to give it a chance. To give *me* a chance. I mean, Jesus Christ, Vicki! You can't work in that goddam booth forever. If you're single, if you're not married—"

"Married?!"

"I don't want to just fuck you, Vicki. I'm sorry. But that's—"

"You're going to get me in trouble, Kevin."

"No, I promise. I'm not."

"You're sure this isn't some kind of weird bullshit, Kevin! To get me into some kind of deep shit with Paul! Because if—"

"Vicki, I swear, I don't know Paul. I've never even heard of him. I give you my word you won't get in any trouble. I don't even know why he sent—"

"You don't?"

"I mean I know why you came here, but I don't know how this guy Paul got—Vicki, look, whatever happened or didn't happen, it's all just between you and me, I swear it. If anyone—"

She was buttoning her blouse again. Her crimson fingernails were like angry comets swirling among trackless rhinestone stars.

"—you can just tell him we spent the entire night fucking our—"

"Ha!" Now she was seizing her fuchsia overcoat from the armchair, hurling it about her shoulders. The tattered pelts of dead white rabbits scampered limply about the fringe.

She strode to the front door, yanked it open, whirled to face him. "You'll at least pay for my cab fare, right?" she glowered.

"Sure," mumbled Kevin uncomfortably. "How—"

"Twenty-seven dollars."

"Jesus Christ, Vicki! Where's this cab taking you to? Mars?"

"Fuck you, Kevin!" she shrieked at him. "Just fuck you! At this fucking hour, I am not taking the fucking subway to Queens, Kevin! And if you fucking think I am—"

Kevin reached into his pocket, fished out three tens. "Got change?" he asked her.

She tore open her purse, cursorily glancing inside it, then snatched the tens from Kevin's grasp and whirled out the door. "This better not turn out to be some kind of asshole Mickey Mouse bullshit you're playing on me, Kevin!"

Then the wrought-iron gate clanged shut behind her and she vanished. Nighttime, that great shadowy hippopotamus, had swallowed her whole.

Kevin snatched up the phone and dialed Guido Gallante. It had rung four times before an inadvertent glance at the Cat's Paw clock reminded him that it was 1:30 AM.

"Hello?" The voice sounded torpid, lethargic, slightly stupefied, but with Guido it was hard to tell whether that meant he'd been asleep or awake.

"Jesus, Guido, I'm—I'm sorry!" exclaimed Kevin. "I guess I forgot it was—"

"Hey, no sweat, Kev," came the reply. "Forget it." There was a pause. "The bimbo. Is she still—"

"No," Kevin replied. "She just left."

"Oh, jeez, Kev. I'm sorry. I mean it. I put in for the all-nighter, Kev. Honest to god. But a lot of 'em just won't do it. They're scared stiff of what somebody might do to 'em after they fall—"

"No, Guido, wait!" interjected Kevin. "She didn't refuse anything. I sent—"

"Oh, fuck! You're not going to tell me I fucked up, are you, Kevin? You're not going to tell me I had 'em send out the wrong—"

"Guido, listen to me! You—"

"Because all I had was that little synopsis you gave me, remember? Up at Dynamic? And from—"

"Guido, relax! You were perfect! Magic! For the life of me, I can't even imagine how you—"

"Magic? You mean I got the right girl?"

"Yes, Guido! Perfect! She—"

"She showed up on your doorstep? She laid that red snapper on you? The two of—"

"Well, no," stammered Kevin, "not exactly. Because—"

"This ain't gonna be like charades, is it, Kevin, at one-fuckin'-thirty in the morning?"

"Hunh—?!"

"You're not gonna make me stand here and ask you forty-seven different questions before I get to find out how come I send you out some choice pussy, gratis, and now you are hemming and hawing at me at fucking two o'clock in the—"

"Guido, it was the right girl," blurted Kevin, "and it was really great what you did, and if it's anyone's fault it's my fault for not—"

"Can you just spit it out, Kev?"

"I don't want just to fuck her."

Guido Gallante paused incredulously. "Okay, you've got my attention, Kevin. What is it you *do* want to do with her?"

Kevin sucked in his breath. "I want to take her out on a date."

"You want to go on a date with a whore?"

Kevin bit his lip.

"You know what *Shinola* is, Kevin?"

"No."

"It's a brand of shoe polish they used to have around when I was a kid. You don't know shit from it, Kevin."

"Guido, I—"

"What the fuck kinda date you wanta take her on, Kevin? Carnegie Hall? The opera? The fucking Bronx Zoo?"

"The Dynamic Christmas party."

"What?!"

CHAPTER 25

▼

Whichever way he looked at her, she blinded him. She was a mirror-maze of diamonds cut to bedazzling brightness ... glittery shards of blasted windshield glass strewn on a highway ... a coruscating shower of galaxial light. Kevin screwed his eyes shut, and by the time he reopened them the silver-sequined gown she wore had metamorphosed again, into shimmering cataracts of fireflies, a simoom of stars.

The party was going full tilt when they got there. Liveried waiters and waitresses bustled about the starkly shadowed disco-lit restaurant serving up canapés to the four hundred famished freelance guests, and a harshly amplified rock band inflicted itself on the proceedings with such raucous intensity that thinking was difficult and ordinary conversation all but ruled out.

Not counting the drinks and hors d'oeuvres, and the gargantuan specially prepared cake with its intricately iced, multi-hued tableau depicting a crowded swarm of Dynamic's heroes hurtling outward toward the viewer—or eater—in awe-inspiring super-powered flight, the food for the occasion was available solely from the long banks of glass-fronted, coin-operated, sandwich-sized serving compartments for which this restaurant, the last surviving Horn & Hardart Automat in New York City, was so justifiably renowned, and which, for tonight only, had been denuded of their customary cafeteria-style offerings—

which, incidentally, Kevin adored—and restocked with the tepid pasta salads and artsy-fartsy *nouvelle cuisine* which appealed irresistibly to the ultrararefied gourmet tastes of the Dragon Lady but which everyone else in the world of comic books loathed.

To her everlasting good credit, however, the Dragon Lady was not consigning her invited celebrants to buying their own food. Attractive, if somewhat boyishly proportioned female models, garbed as Santa's elves, circulated through the throng of partygoers, doling out little gold-net bags bulging with complimentary shiny brass tokens for the food slots, while the reliably inebriated Ed Scanlon, clad in his own jolly rented red Santa suit, lumbered lecherously after them, swilling Johnny Walked Red and tweaking the elves' tight behinds whenever he could get close to them.

When Kevin was a boy, there had been half a dozen of these Automats in Manhattan. As often as he dared, and always under cover of some errand, his father would drive him in from New Jersey and they'd sneak off to one of them, first purchasing a few dollars' worth of nickels from the cashier—she had this uncanny way of flinging fistfuls of nickels toward you across her marble countertop that unerringly added up to the exact amount you'd requested from her—and then fanning out among the banks of tiny food compartments, with their bronze fittings and round porcelain-capped knobs and brightly lighted glass windows showcasing the tantalizing array of edible junk inside.

The foods were all *verboten* ones for Kevin's father, whose diet was tightly prescribed because of his heart condition. Kevin's mother guarded her husband's diet like a hawk. If she'd had any inkling of what he ate at the Automat, she'd probably have had a heart attack herself. Their peach and cherry pies were his father's favorites. He always bought himself a slice of each, devouring them in tandem with two scoops of ice cream, a forkful of slurpy cherry followed by a forkful of peach. And every time they did it, his father had made him swear not to tell—inculpatory oaths which had made him an accomplice in his father's death.

He glanced quickly to his right now, almost to assure himself that she was actually there, that she was a flesh-and-blood person and not some taunting mirage. A hundred ravenous male eyes bore out of the surrounding strobe-lit darkness to transfix her like tractor beams as they strode to the bar. Bathed in the transmogrifying glow of revolving discothèque light, Vicki's sequined gown became a glowing chameleon's skin of amber, lavender, and neon green. Her blond hair became an iridescent corona of finely spun glass. Guido Gallante, mused Kevin silently, was an inspired genius, even though he'd made it clear that this was a first-and-last-time favor and that after tonight he was on his own.

."Not planning on hogging her all to yourself, are you, Kevin?" shouted a too-familiar voice over the cacophonous din of the music.

Kevin looked up from his Coke to find himself face to face with Solly Bernstein, regally turned out in a plush dark-brown velvet suit set off by a raucously loud too-wide tie and hauling along, in his wake, two anemically pale, effeminate young men bedecked in black leather from head to toe and festooned with bike chains and intimidating leather wristlets adorned with ferocious metal studs. One wore his hair in a puke-green Mohawk, while his companion's coiffure thrust aggressively outward from his scalp in a savage cluster of angry spikes.

"Hi, I'm Solly Bernstein," proclaimed Bernstein with randy cordiality, his eyeballs fastened like new Velcro onto Vicki's breasts. "And these are the two Tuttles, Andy and Sandy. You know their stuff, right, Kevin? They're the guys who've been doing *Samurai Armadillo Newshawks* for Cloud Comix."

"Oh, sure," nodded Kevin exaggeratedly, realizing that his voice would be only thinly audible over the din, "I know it. I caught the first four issues—thought they were great! I'm Kevin Ellman, and this—"

"Oh, you don't have to tell us who *you* are," interjected the Mohawk Tuttle deferentially. "We practically cut our first teeth on your *Shambler*, didn't we, Andy?"

"You can say that again," grinned the spiked Tuttle enthusiastically.

"Who did you say your friend was?" leered Bernstein impatiently.

"Vicki," she volunteered, her eyes in her drink.

"Vicki who?" prodded Bernstein.

"Just Vicki," she repeated.

Bernstein shrugged. "Andy and Sandy are going to be here through the holidays," he went on. "I was thinking—"

"My face needs some work, Kevin, okay?" interrupted Vicki. "I'm going to the girls' room. Hold my drink, okay?"

The silvery ankle-length dress was tight. The Tuttles were indifferent, but Bernstein ogled her rapaciously as she minced away, raising a velvet sleeve to his forehead to soak up the sweat. "Whew! Edible, Kevin!" he hyperventilated. "Is she in fuck films?"

Kevin shook his head.

"You're sure?" chimed in Sandy ingenuously. "She certainly would look miraculous in fuck films!"

"If Kevin says no, it's no," exclaimed Bernstein cheerfully, clapping Kevin hard on the shoulder in an exaggerated gesture of camaraderie. "Kevin and I are the fucking experts around here, right, Kevin?"

"Right," replied Kevin, clearing his throat and using his breast-pocket handkerchief to blot some spilled drink from his lapel.

"All the same," Bernstein concluded, "she—uh-oh, we better get going. The party's half over and I promised I'd introduce these guys around. Take it easy, Kevin, right? Maybe we can get together sometime during the holidays."

Kevin waved at them and they were gone. The earsplitting death rock had at last subsided, even if the respite was only temporary. He was about—

"Any guesses who I'm supposed to be?" a deep voice boomed in his ear.

It was Ed Scanlon in his Santa suit, his stocking cap already misplaced among the merrymakers, his fake beard askew. "Can you guess who I'm supposed to be?" he repeated absurdly, cradling his half-depleted bottle of scotch adoringly in the crook of one arm.

"Sure," replied Kevin brightly, striving, as best he could, to enter into the good-natured inebriated inanity of it all. "You're—"

"SANTA CLAUS!!" roared Scanlon boisterously, pounding his thigh mirthfully and then hastening to reward himself for his gigantic comedic endeavor with a long, slow pull on his bottle of scotch. "I'VE CRASHED THIS IDIOTIC GODFORSAKEN FUCKING PARTY DISGUISED AS—SHH!—DISGUISED—SHH!—AS SANTA CLAUS!!" And then Scanlon began cackling and hooting so loudly and insanely that Kevin was fearful he would never stop.

Then suddenly Kevin spotted Vicki threading her way toward him through the partying throng. She had a happy smile on her face in place of the faintly petulant, sullen expression she'd been wearing from the moment she'd picked him up at his house in a cab. The instant she drew near, Scanlon's entire demeanor changed and his maniacal drunken laughter ceased. It was typical of Scanlon, in fact, that he invariably left Kevin wondering whether he was really as snookered as he liked to seem.

"Well, hello there, young lady!" he exclaimed expansively, bowing gallantly, if a bit unsteadily, while simultaneously shifting his phony beard into proper face-front position with a decisive yank on its elastic band. "I'm—"

"I know who you are," she scolded him, trying hard to sound stern and reproachful but giving herself away by giggling, "but whoever heard of Santa running around the North Pole trying to fuck all his little elves?"

"Well, uh, you see, my dear," intoned Scanlon, shifting his weight in a show of simulated guiltiness from one foot to the other while his rheumy gray eyes sparkled mischievously, "officially, by which I mean, uh, geophysically speaking, this is not really the North Pole and, uh, those gracile nymphs you call elves...." Scanlon trailed off into reflective silence, refueling himself with another long, slow pull on his scotch.

For the first time that evening, Vicki leaned close against Kevin and clasped his arm. "Kevin, who's Dream Lass?" she whispered softly.

"Dream Lass?" answered Kevin. "She's—"

"Kevin!" called out Naomi Fenster, the Dragon Lady's administrative assistant, suddenly, rushing toward them clutching a while envelope in one hand. "I've been scouring this place for you. The Shambler screening's been moved up. I wanted to make sure you got your tickets. You'll be able to make it, won't you, Kevin?"

Kevin opened the flap of the proffered envelope, peeked inside. "I'll be there, no problem," he replied.

"It would be just awful if Kevin couldn't come," exclaimed Fenster, turning toward Vicki with a gesture of supreme relief. "I mean, after all, Kevin is practically the star!"

"Star?" queried Vicki, as Fenster scurried away.

"Well, not 'star' exactly," demurred Kevin modestly. "I—"

"Now hold on just a fucking minute there, Kevin!" boomed out Scanlon exuberantly, reentering the conversation for Kevin's benefit. "This 'star' business really isn't too far off the bat! Our Kevin here is an absolutely world-class wordsmith! He single-handedly created the Shambler, which is now being made into a major Hollywood—"

"Kevin, I remember that now!" exclaimed Vicki, brightening. "Didn't you tell me about it one day in the boo—"

"Yes!" interjected Kevin hastily, clearing his throat. "But I think—"

"Kevin, we could dance, couldn't we?" she asked him, draining her drink glass and setting it down on the bar.

"Uh, yes, why don't you," intoned Scanlon somberly, clutching his bottle, reeling away. "It's high time I got back anyway to checking on the whereabouts of those, ahem, elves."

The band had resumed playing now and was kicking off with a medley of slow numbers designed for the over-fifty set. Rather than put up a struggle about dancing altogether, Kevin practically dragged her to the dance floor, reasoning that he'd be wiser to get his ordeal over with before the tempo of the music abruptly changed.

"Who's Dream Lass, Kevin?" she asked him again once they'd reached the dance floor.

He loved having her in his arms, and there was a radiant glow emanating from deep within her face that he'd never seen before in the booth. He was harboring second thoughts about those sequins, though. Dazzling as they were to look at—

"Kevin, who's—"

—pressed against his palms, they had the discomforting reptilian texture of a crocodile's skin.

"C'mon, Kevin! Tell me who—"

"Dream Lass? She's one of Dynamic's comic book characters. Why?"

"Is she gorgeous? Do I look like her?"

"Not half as gorgeous as you, Vicki."

She punched him playfully on the shoulder. "C'mon, is she?"

"Absolutely gorgeous! She'll take your breath away!"

"Wanta know why I wanta know?"

Kevin looked into her eyes and nodded. Of course he wanted to know.

"Because when I went to the ladies' room, this man...." Her eyes cast about the room, trying to search out the man she was so eager to tell Kevin about. And Kevin's eyes followed hers, endeavoring to anticipate whom she was looking for. At the outer edge of the dance floor, Ron Hinder was dancing a slow fox-trot with the Dragon Lady. On festive occasions like these, the Dragon Lady could be a flamboyant dresser, but Hinder had her plainly outclassed tonight in his raspberry-red summertime slacks and eye-blinding Hawaiian shirt with purple-and-orange orchid print. His shoulder-length reddish-brown hair was pulled back in a ponytail held in place with a wide black velvet bow. And just beyond Hinder, lurking motionless and alone in the shadows at the edge of the dance floor, stood Octavia, her curly dark-brown hair cut stylishly short, watching him, jealous of him, at least Kevin would have sworn she was. Fuck Octavia, he thought, and pulled Vicki tightly—

"There!" she exclaimed softly. "There!"

Kevin darkened. Her gleaming red fingernail was directed straight at Ron Hinder. "That's Ron Hinder," he said flatly. "My editor. What—"

"He came up to me after I left the ladies' room. He said he knew I was a friend of yours, and that they were looking for a girl to play the part of Dream Lass at their next convention, and that if—"

At that very instant, Hinder looked up and, spotting Kevin, flashed him an enthusiastic thumb's up. Kevin felt suddenly ridiculous and ashamed.

"Did you hear me, Kevin?"

"Yes," he answered her, "of—"

"A thousand dollars, Kevin! Five hundred dollars a day for two whole days! And all I have to do is—"

"You'll be great at it," Kevin reassured her warmly. "You should do it."

"But that is all I'd have to do, right, Kevin?"

"Sure."

"They wouldn't expect me to—"

"Uh-uh," answered Kevin with an indulgent smile. "Nothing. Greet visitors to their hospitality suite. Hand out a few flyers. Maybe let some kids snap—"

"Your creation being made into a movie, Kevin! This modeling job! I didn't understand before—"

"Understand?"

"—that you were so important."

CHAPTER 26

▼

His beloved monster looked pathetic, and whoever had designed that giant scorpion could only have been a blithering moron, but there they were, duking it out in front of a painted Himalayan backdrop amid what looked to be a blizzard of soap flakes, the giant scorpion looking for all the world like a mammoth pincered waterbed, the Shambler lurching stiffly about in bug-eyed goggles and a scaly wetsuit, like some gloppy retread from the *Black Lagoon*.

"Kevie, you're a genius," whispered Vicki softly in the darkness. "I'm so proud to be here with you."

How can she say that? he wondered bewilderedly to himself. How could she even think it? Could she actually be so blissfully unmindful of the terrible shame and humiliation he felt? Was she so bedazzled by her fantasies of his wealth and celebrity that she had become literally blinded to what she saw on the screen?

"Kevie!" she cooed at him again, and in the flickering blackness, she kissed him gently on his squirrel face and squeezed his hand.

The Shambler, meantime, was still locked in combat with the giant scorpion—and definitely getting the worst of it. He heaved a papier-mâché boulder at his arachnid adversary, but the scorpion scuttled aside in the nick of time and the boulder plopped harmlessly amid the pillow-soft drifts of ivory snow. And then abruptly the scorpion's tail emitted an incandescent spark, unquestionably the most ambitious special effect thus far, and the mighty snow man clapped his hands to his head and emitted an earsplitting Tarzan-inspired bellow of pain.

Kevin gnawed his lip and averted his embarassed eyes from the screen. Fidgeting uncomfortably in his seat, he glanced hastily around the screening room, trying to discern whether anyone else felt as humiliated as he did. If they did, however, they were contriving to keep their emotions well hidden. The Dragon Lady sat impassively in her armchair, eyes fixed on the screen. Ron Hinder sprawled shamelessly beside her, like a whore in bed, dutifully witnessing the debacle—or was he perhaps sound asleep?—through lavender-tinted eyeglasses more suitable for sunbathing on Miami Beach. A clutch of sharkskin-suited movie executives, whom Kevin had never laid eyes on before, looked on with the supercilious complacency of men whose sole criterion of cinematic achievement was that the film be completed under budget and on time.

The scorpion lay dying now, dispatched by some no-doubt-brilliant stratagem that Kevin had evidently missed. Its scarifying pincers click-clacked ever more feebly in the snow, requiring only minor readjustments before they were brought back for a reprise performance in some grade-Z pterodactyl-laden film.

The Shambler's tribulations, however, were far from over. The huge-breasted archvillainess behind the scorpion now made her malevolent grand entrance, austerely indifferent to the sub-zero Himalayan cold despite being clad in nothing more than a skintight scoop-necked black leather dress.

Vicki was wearing a tight black leather miniskirt and a V-necked gold blouse that shimmered as though it had been spun from metallic strands. And now she had slipped one foot free of its ankle-length gold boot and was rubbing it provocatively up and down against his leg.

By this time Kevin was geared to expect the absolute worst. He was expecting the leather-clad villainess to propose a truce, to suggest that she and the Shambler join forces to conquer the earth and rule it together, side by side.

The rubbing of Vicki's foot was becoming more insistent now, and coital low moans, like the ones he was so accustomed to hearing from phone sex, were issuing from the back of her throat. For a split instant, Kevin became petrified that the Dragon Lady might hear them, and then he realized he secretly hoped that she did. Without once taking his eyes off the movie screen, he swiveled around partway in his armchair and lay his palm firmly against the inside of Vicki's thigh. Only then, with his perspiring fingers straining to awkwardly reconnoiter the dizzyingly erotic no-man's-land inside her miniskirt, did Kevin realize that she was wearing real stockings and garters, not pantyhose, and that if she owned any panties, she had left them at home. The armchairs were bolted to the floor, so he couldn't move closer to her, but she slipped down slightly in her seat and spread her thighs wide to open herself up to him.

The Shambler seemed either curious or undecided, it was hard to tell which. He shuffled diffidently toward the temptress, who made ready to enfold him in an erotic embrace.

Kevin thrust his hand upward along the soft flesh of Vicki's inner thigh—and found himself clutching a dewy fistful of muff. He twisted his wrist—she hoisted herself upward in her seat to assist him, ever so slightly—and plunged his middle finger deep into the fastness of her oozing wet cunt. "Oohhh!" she sighed ecstatically, and clutched his arm.

With a breath-stopping gasp, Kevin remembered the poisoned lipstick. In his excitement, he'd nearly forgotten how she'd used it to dispatch a faithless henchman early in the film. And—dear god! no!—the Shambler was actually about to kiss her!

"NO!!" shrieked Kevin at the top of his lungs. "DON'T!!"

Good god! Had he really screamed that? No. Wait. Perhaps he hadn't. Or if he had, they hadn't heard him. Not one of the other swiveling armchairs whirled to reprimand him.

The long, slender fingers of her right hand were stroking his cock now, urgently stroking his hard penis through the dark blue wool of his pants. Her fingernails had been repainted gold to coordinate with her shoes, her hair, her blouse. Her vagina slurped at his middle finger like a famished little mouth.

"Kevin! Please!" she whispered thickly, huskily. "I want you to take me home and fuck me!"

Kevin worked his hand free from between her thighs and swiveled round to the empty seat close by, where he'd piled their coats. The coat chair shrieked like a startled banshee when he touched it, but not a soul in the screening room whirled to reproach him. Somehow he and Vicki had warped through an ethereal portal into an alternate universe where he could scream his head off if he wanted to, and only she would be able to hear him.

*   *   *   *

And yet his right shoulder blade was throbbing like crazy. It began when they left the screening room and got progressively worse, so that by the time they exited the cab in front of his apartment building, Kevin was practically doubled over with pain. All he could think of was, Oh my god! What will she do to me if it turns out I can't fuck her?

With Vicki close beside him, he wrenched open his apartment door and switched on the pole lamp. Its anarchic beams hacked up the room. The New Guinea spirit mask glowered malevolently from the wide brick wall. Don't worry, it promised, I'll frighten her off for you.

In the bathroom medicine cabinet, Kevin unearthed a half-empty bottle of librium, the remnants of a tranquilizer prescription provided by his doctor at the height of his marital difficulties with Eugènie. He gulped down a pair of the blue-green capsules, fervently praying he'd be able to stall Vicki until they began to work.

By the time he stepped back out into the living room she was half-undressed—her fuchsia overcoat draped over the armchair, her spun-gold blouse on the couch—and with the gangly gracefulness of a newborn peroxide colt she was stepping free of her leather skirt. His arousal dully muted by the throbbing ache in his shoulder blade, Kevin almost numbly followed suit. She stood there now, semi-nude, pert breasts exposed, clad only in sheer black stockings and a black lace garter belt. Her muff hair was a soft light brown, like the soothing bristles of his father's shaving brush. What was she doing here? he wondered. Why hadn't she been repelled by the scars that the squirrel of his childhood had gnawed on his face?

"… down, Kevin?"

"Huh-!?"

"You heard me."

"No, honest," he stammered. "I-I didn't."

"I want you to take it down," she repeated.

"What down?"

"That," she pointed. "The voodoo thing."

Kevin's delay was no more than the length of a heartbeat.

"I don't want it to be able to watch us."

"I've got a bedroom," Kevin answered her. "We'll close the door."

She followed him into the bedroom, circumnavigating his paper junk piles and stretching herself out full-length on the bed. Kevin knelt above her, facing her, straddling her thighs, then extended his body out over hers, his weight on his left forearm, and plunged his long, hard penis deep inside her cunt. Only then did it even dawn on him that he hadn't embraced her in the living room, hadn't kissed her before they started fucking, hadn't even paused to suck her nipples or caress her breasts. He hoped she hadn't noticed, that all the kissing they'd done in the taxicab had been enough. In any case, her eyes were closed now, and there was no sign she was about to reprimand him.

He was moving in and out now, in and out. He wanted her to have a good time, but with most girls it was hard to tell whether they were having a good time or what they were thinking about. Except when they screamed. Octavia used to scream her fucking head off. It had frightened him at first, made him fearful that he was hurting her. It was so hard to tell what was happening, to really know what effect you were having. But at least when they were screaming you knew that they were really there with you, and not somewhere else.

The ridges inside Vicki's vagina were gently thrumming the head of his cock. The sensation excited Kevin, but it also made him worry that he hadn't gotten her wet enough. The tranquilizers weren't working either. His shoulder still throbbed. But at least the pain was distracting him, ensuring that he wouldn't ruin everything by coming too soon.

He looked down at her face, and found himself focusing on her makeup for what felt like the first time. Worn and smudged by all that kissing in the cab, it suddenly seemed like a false face, a mask, designed to prevent him from discovering who she really was. Only now he was peering through the mask, glimpsing the face of an ordinary twenty-three or twenty-four-year-old girl.

The girls in the porno mags he read were perfect. From the glistening pinkness of their beavers to the tawdry sensuality of their lingerie, they represented a kind of erotic chalice that men like Kevin sought and longed for. But what if it were all a mask of some kind—a fraud, an art form? What if—and this was not the first time this particular unsettling thought had occurred to Kevin—there really were no women like that in the world?

Vicki had opened her blue-green eyes now and was looking up at him, peering out at him from behind the decomposing mask. Had she come yet? He could almost never tell unless they told him, and even then he was never certain whether he could really believe them or not. Was she perhaps impatient with him because he hadn't come yet? Furious with him for some reason he couldn't even suspect? And why was that muscle in his shoulder blade torturing him the way it was? Where did that nagging feeling come from that he'd somehow gotten something he wasn't supposed to have?

It seemed to him that he probably ought to come now. Even with Octavia, the first time hadn't been the best. He flashed back to Vicki stroking his cock through his pants in the screening room. In his mind's eye he unzipped his fly and she knelt down in front of him and began to suck. God, wouldn't that have been incredible? Fuck Ron Hinder! Fuck the Dragon Lady!

And then some obscure gear clicked in Kevin's brain and it was *Octavia's* mouth, *Octavia* kneeling in front of him in the screening room, sucking his cock till he was on the very brink of coming—and then abruptly scuttling away from him to suck off Jean-Claude Allande on the other side of the aisle! She scuttled along sideways, dragging herself across the screening-room carpet with arms that terminated in the pincers of a giant crab! And then—

Only a Herculean mental effort enabled Kevin to wrench himself back to the present. Vicki was his woman now. He wanted to ejaculate a huge foaming gusher of semen inside of her. He wanted to give her— *a baby!*

And then all at once—good god!—he was in the hospital, in the delivery room of a god damn hospital, and he was lying face up on the delivery table, surrounded by doctors and nurses, yes and Vicki in a surgical mask and hospital gown, he felt fine except for the throbbing in his shoulder, that and the strange pressure between his—

BRINGGGGG!

—legs, but whose godawful little head was that, all bloody—

BRINGGGGG!

BRINGGGGG!

The ringing telephone was like a hammered spike in his brain.

BRINGGGGG!

His shoulder throbbed unmercifully, and he knew he wouldn't be able to make himself come right now even if his life—

BRINGGGGG!

"Will it make you angry if I answer it?" he asked her.

BRINGGGGG!

"No, why?" she replied. "Go ahead."

It was Ora, calling from Seattle. She was planning on flying in over the weekend and wanted to make sure he'd be able to meet with her. "Sure," Kevin assured her, and hung up.

"Who was that woman, Kevin?"

"How—"

"Don't try to mind-fuck with me, Kevin. Who—"

"Ora," interjected Kevin hastily. "My sister. She's flying in from the Coast at the end of the week and she wants to—"

"Wants what?"

"—to have a long heart-to-heart talk with me about death."

CHAPTER 27

▼

By the time she finally got around to the commercial, they were being menaced by the jaws of Carboniferous sharks.

"... auction off the entire collection now, while the market for those nineteenth-century romantic pastoralists is artificially high."

"I don't think she needs the money, Ora."

"That's not exactly the point, Kevin." She paused. "In a long-term sense, it's our money, too."

They had wandered into a high-vaulted basilica of ancient undersea life, helpless prey to the mammoth cartilaginous skeletons of long-extinct fish.

"When I said I'd enjoy meeting at a museum, Kevin, I didn't exactly mean this one."

"I like this one. And besides, it's not far from my house."

"Still hooked on dinosaurs, aren't you, Kevin? Still just a little boy."

"Now you sound like Eugènie," smiled Kevin.

"You could've done a lot worse," retorted Ora. But her brother was elsewhere, hoping that when it was finally identified, the Loch Ness monster would turn out to be a race of plesiosaurs.

"You were a jerk to fuck around on her, Kevin."

"What should she buy instead, Sis?"

"You mean to replace Dad's pastoralists?"

Kevin nodded.

"Abstractionsists. Going to start selling like hotcakes. There are a whole slew of *petits maîtres* out there she could pick up for practically nothing."

"You mean second stringers?"

Ora winced disdainfully.

"They might be nice, Ora, but they wouldn't be Dad's paintings."

"Are you really so certain she even likes those paintings?"

"I think she likes them because they were Dad's."

There had been a whole genre of comic books in the 1960s featuring platoons of square-jawed GIs fighting it out with dinosaurs in mysterious mist-enshrouded valleys that time forgot. Kevin stumbled upon them occasionally at conventions or in the bargain bins at comics shops, and it never failed to make him sick to look at them.

"It's as though he were still alive and kicking, isn't it, Kevin?"

"What?!" asked Kevin.

"Just listen to the two of us trying to carry on a conversation like this, in a museum no less, where you have to keep your voices low—just like we always had to do around the house when we were kids, remember? And even today, here, when we're trying to come to some rational decision about something, the boundaries are *his* boundaries, the parameters of everything have been fixed by Dad."

Kevin blinked uncomfortably. "No," he stammered, "I don't think I—"

"Oh, for christ's sake, Kevin! Don't tell me you've forgotten how much we both hated him for being so sick—how we resented the million ways in which his heart condition circumscribed our lives!"

Kevin's eyes had begun burning, but he wasn't sure why.

"Don't you remember that time when you were twelve and I was five and a half, and you were playing at conducting auto-safety crash tests with your model cars, and Mom came in and said, 'Keep quiet! Your father—,' and you screamed out, 'Then I wish he would go ahead and die already so that at least Ora and I could act like real kids and make some decent noise around here!' and she smacked your face so hard your teeth were rattling for a week?"

CHAPTER 28

▼

"Kevin?"

"Vicki? Is—"

"Damn it, where've you been, Kevin? I've been calling and—"

"My sister, remember? I just—"

"I can't stay there anymore, Kevin. I never thought he was really serious—you know what I mean?—but he was! Now I don't know what the fuck—"

"Stay? Stay where?"

"Aw, c'mon, Kevie, come back to the mother planet, will you, honey? Haven't you been listening to what I've been telling you? I've been kicked out of my apartment, Kevie! The land—"

"But why?"

"Fuck, I don't know, Kevin! Because he's a *landlord*, that's why! I don't know why the fuck those shitty—"

"Do you need a place to stay?" he asked her.

Pause.

"Because if you do, you know you can—"

Pause.

"Vicki?"

"Oh, Kevie, I don't know if—"

"You know what I want you to do," he whispered to her. "And—"

An altercation exploded in the background, abruptly dampened by a slamming door.

"Vicki, where—"

"Work."

"Want to sit tight and let me—"

"No, baby. No. Trish can help pile me into a—"

"Cab?"

"Uh-huh. Listen, Kevie, I'm going to go now. Twenty minutes, though, okay?"

Kevin hung up the telephone as eddies of anxiety and exhilaration fluttered through him like a chilling wind. Hastily shoveling some wayward outcroppings of comics stacks into a corner, he momentarily contemplated taking down the spirit mask, decided against it, and then threw on his winter coat and dashed outside. And when she spilled out of her taxicab forty-five minutes later, weighed down by a pair of mismatched vinyl suitcases and a cavernous white leather drawstring bag, he feverishly thrust a ten-dollar bill through the driver's window and then rushed around to the curb side to help Vicki with her bags.

"I don't understand," exclaimed Kevin, shouldering open his apartment door and setting the bags down on the living-room floor. "Your apartment. How could—"

"Kevin, I don't want to talk about that now," she pouted.

"Uh, okay," stammered Kevin, intimidated. "What do—"

"You'll see!" she retorted, brightening flirtatiously and swirling toward the bathroom door with her drawstring bag. "Last time, you wouldn't let me do anything! This time, I'm going to fuck your brains out!"

When she emerged moments later, she was wearing high-heeled shoes, mesh hose, and a domino face mask and bikini fashioned out of soft, downy, lavender-and-black feathers. The mask's eyeholes were edged with gold sequins complementing the latticework of matching sequins that made up the bikini's crotch. Kevin looked, and for a fleeting instant, imagined himself as a fox with a doughnut of bloodstained lavender poultry feathers encircling his mouth.

"You're not laughing at me, are you, Kevin?" she asked him, her expression saucy but her voice tinged ever so slightly with self-doubt.

"No, of course not," he smiled at her, and opened his arms wide to embrace her. The feathers were scratchy, even through the cloth of his Shambler T-shirt, and her costume looked more than a little bit foolish. But the dawning notion that she had become somehow vulnerable to him, that what she wanted was to tap into his deepest sexual fantasies and indulge them, was almost more unnervingly pleasurable to him than he could bear. He plunged both hands into the back of her panties, clutching her firm, tight buttocks in two fists and crushing her crotch up against his so that she could feel the rock-hard bulge of his cock. Her firm, pink mouth locked onto his mouth, and Kevin could feel the faint taste of blood tricking from his lower lip.

He tore off his T-shirt and flung it away from him, then feverishly stripped off his shoes, his slacks, his undershorts and drew her onto the couch.

He got her mask off first, although not without knotting the shoestring bow that held it on her into an intractable mess, then gripped awkwardly at her panties, trying desperately to rip them off.

"Kevin, they're expensive!" she scolded him, and this rebuke frightened him, until she rose to her feet and stepped deftly out of them, the impish look in her eye assurance enough that it wouldn't have mattered if he'd torn them to shreds.

Stretched out nude on the couch, watching as she unhooked her feathered bra and let it drop to the floor, Kevin reached out a hand to grasp her calf and draw her gently toward him, simultaneously shifting onto his side so that when she lay on the couch he'd be in position to climb on top of her.

"Forget it. Not this time," she teased him, coaxing him gently onto his back and lowering herself back onto the sofa to kneel between his legs. "I told you I was going to do you this time, right?"

The free, unrestrained use of his own body was all but impossible for Kevin—although in the sex act he somehow became more relaxed and uninhibited than at any other time—but total passivity had always been out of the question. The very idea of remaining motionless during sex made him squirm with discomfort, and unnerved him in some subliminal way he did not understand. He shot a glance at the spirit mask, looming over them on the brick wall, and it occurred to him that at any moment now she'd probably notice it and insist that they retreat to the bedroom and shut the door.

But if the mask's watchful gaze unsettled her, she didn't show it. She had her mouth on his testicles now, mouthing and sucking them, and was deftly stroking his cock with the slender fingers of one hand. Then she squeezed the underside of his thigh somehow, and Kevin realized she meant for him to raise his legs. He reached out a hand to softly tousle her hair, while her tongue and lips probed the region beneath his testicles, pausing, now and again, to plant soft kisses at the places where his buttocks sloped into the backs of his thighs. Kevin was trying hard not to let his anxiety run rampant, to distract himself away from his fears with thoughts of how unbelievably happy and excited he was. He was the Shambler, after all, and Vicki was his Golden Starling, sensuous birdwoman princess of—

An acutely disquieting, wholly unfamiliar sensation startled Kevin out of his fantasy. He looked down and—good god!—Vicki had her head down between his legs and was adroitly using her soft, wet tongue to probe the delicate membranes inside his ass.

"NO!" he moaned, but it was as though someone else had moaned it, as though the futile throaty protest had emanated from the primal countenance of woven sago-palm spathe and raffia peering enigmatically down at them from the living-room wall.

The sensory overload was overpowering. It was like the way the head of Kevin's cock always felt right after coming, or like the way women sometimes had said they felt when he'd applied his tongue too strenuously to their clit. But there was a whole lot more to the way he felt now, and Kevin knew it. There was the glorious yet simultaneously terrifying feeling of having been penetrated, and violated, of slipping perilously backward toward some place he was no longer meant to be. And then there was something else, something scary, having to do with that thin, unnerving affinity between love and shit.

Kevin fought the rising panic, and the panic receded, yielding to a tremulous ecstasy so exquisite that he knew his body couldn't long contain it.

"Vicki!" he exhaled hoarsely, and clutched desperately at her platinum tangle of hair. He was trying to roll her over, to somehow end up with her body beneath his, but the couch was narrow, they rolled too far, and hit the living-room floor with a thud.

"Omigod! Vicki! Are you all right?"

"Yes!" she gasped.

He was above her now, kneeling between her open thighs, grasping his moist cock in one hand and ramming it into her. She moaned, and he drew back for a second thrust, slipping out in his excitement and grabbing it and plunging it back into her. Her eyes shone like blue sky, her hair gleamed like phosphorescent gold. And lavender feathers were scattered everywhere, like the blasted remains of paradisaical birds.

Vicki came and so did Kevin. For the first time in his entire life, Kevin screamed when he shot his come.

CHAPTER 29

▼

Kevin would've given his right arm for a Coke, but all they were serving was wine, cheese, and a few bowlfuls of shelled pistachio nuts. On top of that, the effete black-tie throng was chattering on about comic books as though they'd invented them in a supercilious vocabulary he could not understand, so that what should have been a celebratory tribute to what he and his friends were doing had turned instead into a crashing bore. If this had been the Metropolitan, he could at least have fled to the lobby to daydream those great lance-wielding knights on horseback into a chivalrous joust, but here at the Whitney, where he had never been, there was really nowhere to go, and the exquisitely mounted exhibition of *The Comics as Art,* newly transplanted here after six months at the Louvre, formed, at least, a kind of protective cocoon, insulating him against unwanted aesthetic assault in the roomsful of anarchic contemporary artwork beyond.

Vicki was with him, and looking edible in raspberry spandex tights with matching spike-heeled shoes and a shimmering sea-green top, but she was impatient to leave, and she kept threatening to "get shit-faced on Thunderbird or whatever the fuck this shit is" if he didn't hurry up with his obligatory socializing and get her the hell out of there. She had returned to the wine table, in fact, and lined up for another refill, when Kevin spotted Octavia, alone, on the far side of the room, contemplating a wall-length display of plexiglass frames containing George Pfister's first, crude pencil drawings of Power Man.

She was a tall girl, Octavia—about five-feet-ten or eleven—and the first one he could recall who'd ever agreed to go out with him notwithstanding the fact that, in heels, she was taller than he was.

"Is the old man coming?" he asked her.

"Kevin? Oh, hi! You mean George Pfister? We invited him, but no, I don't think so. He said it would make him even more bitter than he is already, seeing these up here. You know, technically he doesn't even own them. He signed them away to Dynamic years ago, along with all his other rights."

"How's France?" asked Kevin.

"France?"

"Jean-Claude Allande. How—"

"Oh, he's fine. He'll be coming over soon, in fact—says he's planning on giving you a call while he's here, maybe try to come up with something you two could do together. He adores your work, Kevin, and he's grateful—"

"He ought to be," winked Kevin puckishly, "after what I—"

"After what you what?"

"—gave him."

Her eyes narrowed slightly. "*It* wasn't yours to give," she retorted coolly.

Something momentarily outside Kevin's field of vision tore hard at his left arm. "Come on, Kevin!" shrieked Vicki angrily in his ear. "We're leaving!"

"Octavia, this is Vicki," offered Kevin embarrassedly, endeavoring, but not very effectively, to stand his ground. "Vicki, I'd like—"

"I *mean* it, Kevin!" screamed Vicki. "*Come on!*"

"Octavia's just been put in charge of Dynamic's new West Coast animation studio," interjected Kevin desperately. "I just wanted to con—"

"Then hurry the fuck up and congratulate her, Kevin! And let's get the piss-fuck out of here!"

"That's really what I wanted to say to you, Octavia," stammered Kevin frantically. "Congratulations on the great—"

"Thank you," smiled Octavia. "It'll just be for a year at first, to see how—"

Octavia's sentence was truncated by the sound of shattering glass. Vicki had venomously hurled her wine glass at a standing sculpture of the Black Bat, and now, having locked both hands around Kevin's arm, was attempting to drag him bodily out of the hall.

"Octavia, I'm sorry!" exclaimed Kevin apologetically. "I—"

"Forget about it, Kevin," Octavia called out, stifling a giggle and flashing him a little-girl goodbye wave. "This party needed a little injection of life in it anyway."

"Mind clueing me in on what all that was about?" inquired Kevin, striving to regain at least a modicum of his courage as they hurtled out onto Madison Avenue and piled into a cab.

"You've fucked her, haven't you, Kevin!"

"What?"

"Don't try to brain-fuck me, Kevin! She has a hot sloshy wet pussy and she gave you the best ass-fucking and cocksucking of your entire goddam life until you met me!"

"Vicki, look—"

"Who the fuck did you think you were in there? Why the fuck were you—"

"What? What was I—"

"I warned you not to try mind-fucking me, Kevin!"

"Vicki, I'm not trying anything. I just—"

"You were fucking around with her, Kevin! In your fucking insect mind—"

"I wasn't!"

"Fuck you weren't, Kevin! I was there! I saw—"

"Dammit, Vicki! I'm a freelance writer! Octavia is, was, the managing editor at Dynamic Comics! All I—"

"Go ahead, then! Tell me you've never fucked her! Tell—"

"All right," admitted Kevin. "I did. But it was a long time ago. She's with someone else now. He lives in France. I-I even practically introduced them. And all I did tonight was congrat—"

"You didn't congratulate her till after I got there! You didn't even remember you were *supposed* to congratulate her till—"

"We exchanged a few pleasantries first, dammit! About the exhibition, about business. But—"

"Then why the fuck did you have to wait till I was stuck off at the bar getting myself another drink?"

It was a good question—Kevin wasn't sure he knew the answer. But his eyes had started burning. And he wished she'd stop yammering away at him—

"Fucking goddam squirrels should've clawed your goddam eyes out!"

—so he'd have time to stop and figure out what was going on.

"Here, dammit!" she shrieked at the top of her lungs. "Right here!"

They'd arrived at the fire hydrant opposite Kevin's brownstone. The cabdriver obediently slammed on his brakes. Vicki bolted out the door on the street side and dashed to the gate, leaving Kevin to fumble awkwardly for his money, inadvertently handing the driver a ten, instead of a five, then abruptly realizing his mistake but by then feeling too embarrassed and discombobulated to ask for change. By the time he'd extricated himself from the taxicab and reached his apartment, it was to find Vicki in the bedroom, furiously flinging clothing and toiletries into a large overnight bag.

"What—what are you doing?" he gasped dumbly.

"Ha! Fat load of shit you care! What does it look like I'm doing?"

"Vicki! Please!" he cried.

"I'm finished—leaving! And the last thing I need is you trying to stop me!"

"Vicki, this is crazy!" he pleaded. "Please—"

"You're a fucking open wound, Kevin! A freaking zippo! A pussy!" The twin latches of the overnight case clacked shut. "If you and your fucking Oc—"

"But I don't care about Octavia!" he begged her. "She—"

"It's finished, asshole! Over! You blew it! Now get the fuck out of my way!"

Her stiletto heels clacked out a vengeful tattoo on the floorboards as she strode harshly across the living room to the door. "Well?!" she shrieked at him angrily, savagely throttling the doorknob, wrenching open the door. "What the fuck's your problem? Aren't you going to get me a cab?"

Kevin ambled numbly after her, down the hallway, out the gate, and down the half-block to Columbus like an obedient Newfoundland dog.

"You don't give a rusty shit if I leave, do you, Kevin?"

"But that's crazy!" he exclaimed shrilly. "Of course I—"

But her arm was already high in the air, waving wildly for a cab. A cruising gypsy driver, spotting her signal from a full block away, careened insanely across three lanes of onrushing traffic in order to out-race a pair of contending medallion cabs to the fare.

"Vicki! Please!" cried Kevin desperately. "Don't go!"

The cabdriver flicked the backseat door latch and the door flew open. Kevin blundered awkwardly forward and scrabbled terrified at her coat sleeve. "I-I love you!" he wailed piteously. "For god's sake!"

"This snoid giving you trouble, lady?" snarled the cabdriver.

Passing Kevin her overnight bag, Vicki pilloried the cabdriver with an icy stare and slammed the cab door so hard the entire side of the taxicab shook. "Take a hike, asshole!" she spat at him.

"Ditsy cunt!" hurled back the cabdriver. And, spewing great angry gouts of pollution, the taxicab hurtled away.

CHAPTER 30

▼

"... usually just so much cold meat, you know what I mean? But I swear, this guy ..."

It was after 3:00 AM and she was busting his balls again, going on and on about some gorgeous hunk who'd patronized her booth today, stayed over an hour and left a twenty-dollar tip. It seemed for the past month she was always trying to get under his skin, if not with some handsome guy, then with something else. Invariably, a fight would start and, once it did, nothing was off-limits as far as she was concerned—neither his squirrel scars nor his masculinity, most certainly not his writer's block. At some appropriately climactic moment, she'd throw something at him, break something, toss some possessions in a suitcase and storm out the door. Then she'd always let him catch up with her, beg her, plead with her into coming back. The lovemaking afterward was always spectacular, the twin ecstasies of love and anger mingled with the dread of loss.

But over this space of weeks, Kevin had begun to weary—of the game of bait and fight, of the bizarre, round-the-clock hours she kept, rarely consistent from one day to the next, and of her vertiginous non-stop careering between two schizophrenic polarities of mood, from starry apogees of manic excitement to dismal nadirs of torpid despair. And it distressed and bewildered him the way things had lately begun disappearing from their accustomed places: marmalade jars full of quarters, replenished in the wake of his loan arrangement with Guido Gallante, the Olivetti portable that he kept stored in the bedroom clothes closet and seldom used. Finally, and he was genuinely ashamed to have discovered this within himself, he hated the fact that she worked at the Pornomart. It invigorated him that she was a slut, and he relished it, but he wanted her to be *his* slut, and not—

"—Octavia's juicy wet pussy!"

"Wha-!?" blinked Kevin.

"Fuck you, Kevin! Just fuck you! You fucking heard me and you fucking well know it!"

"Something about Octavia?" he asked her.

"I warned you, you sonovabitch! But you've been sticking your dick into her hot little asshole again, and I won't stand for it!"

"Octavia's in California, Vicki," protested Kevin evenly. "I haven't seen—"

"You squirrel-faced bastard! You are lying to me! You're lying to me through your mother-fucking teeth!"

"Octavia's living and working in Los Angeles, Vicki. No—"

"LIAR!! YOU'RE A GOD DAMNED—"

"She's in charge of Dynamic's new animation studio, Vicki. Los—"

"SERENA *SAW* YOU!!"

"Who's Serena, Vicki?"

"SERENA AT THE PORNOMART!! SHE'S *PSYCHIC!!* SHE SAW—"

"Your friend Serena's got her head wedged up her asshole, Vicki. Octav—"

Suddenly, Vicki snatched up the TV remote control from off the coffee table and hurled it at Kevin with all her might. Miraculously, it sailed wide, smacking hard against the brick wall, narrowly grazing the spirit mask and clattering to the floor.

"Dammit, Vicki!" cried Kevin, racing anxiously to the brick wall to assess the damage. "That mask's valuable, and I'm respon—"

WHAM!! He heard the front door slam shut. Oh Jesus Christ! he mused peevishly. Not this again!

Nonetheless, he dashed out the door after her, arriving at the end of the hallway just in time to have the iron gate clang shut in his face.

"VICKI!!" he cried out, but she didn't answer him.

Yet he knew for certain that she was out there, within earshot, less than halfway down the block now, deliberately slowing her pace, allowing him time to catch up with her. This time, though, Kevin had decided to call her bluff. This time he was going to let her go.

Back inside his apartment, he collapsed onto his couch and zapped on the TV. The soft-core porn channel was broadcasting its habitual seamy unending round of commercials for escort services, phone sex, and exorbitant high-toll party lines guaranteed to enable you to establish instantaneous simultaneous telephone contact with "up to eight other men just like you." The purveyors of masturbatory phone sex had of late begun soaring to new heights of competitive sleaziness, with ads showcasing high-smut visuals accompanied by sultry voice-overs proclaiming catchy phone-number acronyms ("... just dial 870-SLUT ...") and slogans of such bizarre hyperbolic vulgarity ("... perverse sluts waiting to suck your hot come ...") that even to a tolerant, even receptive audience like Kevin they smacked less of erotica than they did of high camp. No denying, though, that with the exception of the home shopping channels and Public Television's unending biography of Mountbatten, it was the most scintillating fare available for viewing on late-late-night TV.

Nevertheless, after sitting through about an hour of it ("Hi, I'm Tina, and you can taste my tender wet pussy by dialing 999 ..."), Kevin found himself becoming haunted by anxious thoughts. It seemed unbelievable that she'd stay away this long. But what if something horrible had happened to her? What if she'd gotten sick, or injured? What if she'd wandered up Broadway, not exactly the safest avenue at this hour, and gotten raped and strangled by a multiracial gang?

Kevin threw on his coat and raced out the door, straining hard to blot out the gory images of rapine and slaughter swirling in a gruesome dervish inside his head. But where in the name of heaven was he supposed to look for her? He dashed up the block to Central Park West, saw nothing, then reversed direction and sprinted back down the long crosstown block to Columbus. The trendy mannequins in the high-priced boutiques, all done up in frumpy-looking apparel that appealed to women for reasons that no man could tell, regarded him melancholily from behind padlocked metal window grates and shatter-proof plate glass. One toney emporium, reveling in a prosperity this season beyond all belief, had garnered its fashion inspirations for spring from the black-swathed ninja assassins of feudal Japan. But except for the tireless Korean grocers, mechanically uncrating the next day's produce in the middle of the next block, there wasn't a single living soul in sight.

Not without trepidation, Kevin executed a sharp diagonal across Columbus, turning west on Seventy-second Street and negotiating the lengthy double-block to Broadway at a dead run—racing past the savings and loan and the bathroom boutique, the takeout sushi bar and the fancy choclatier, and finally the organic grocery store, representing the last safe, desperate outpost between the upwardly mobile world of the Upper West Side elite and the demimondain twilight of addicts, pushers, and derelicts.

At the bustling intersection of Seventy-second and Broadway, taxicabs swarmed around the all-night papaya juice and hotdog stand like yellowjackets, black junkies feverishly hawked their scavenged and stolen wares, and a set of double pay phones had had their gray receivers violently severed from their gleaming connective cables, like a bionic man who'd had his hands amputated at the wrists.

Kevin cast his eyes desperately about for Vicki, while guilt seeped corrosively through his vitals like chemical waste. Where was she? he interrogated himself frantically. WHERE WAS SHE? And at 4:30 in the morning, where in god's name could he go to look for her?

Then his ear caught the emphysemic sputter of the downtown bus lurching along Broadway like some timeless armored colossus creaking forth from its darksome chasm to answer the call to battle of a valiant medieval knight. Kevin dashed across the street to the bus stop and leaped on board, knowing the bus would let him off a block from the Pornomart.

The great sleaze mecca was open when he got there, indeed it was always open, but in these grimy predawn hours, when all but the most diehard onanistic denizens were home asleep, or trying to sleep, and only a ragged gaggle of vacant-eyed devotees still roved the amusements on the Pornomart's four floors, the entire establishment struck Kevin less as a gaunt whore, bedizened in glitter and colored lights, than as the putrescent corpse of a ritualistically garroted transvestite already denuded by vermin and hook-beaked birds of but her last few tatters of decomposing flesh.

Kevin shuffled anxiously about the place, glancing furtively from side to side as he went, all but certain that Vicki wasn't here but knowing of no other place where he might search for her. Fearful he'd be challenged for not spending any money, he purchased a few dollars' worth of tokens from a house cashier and wandered aimlessly about, his face averted to avoid confronting the intimidating gaze of the house security men.

Arriving at the booth where Vicki worked, and noting that the red light atop the adjoining patron's booth was lit, Kevin paused there awhile and waited, hanging far enough back from the rotunda's edge to render it unlikely that he'd be accosted directly by girls lounging in front of any of the other booths. A quarter-hour passed, and still the red booth-light remained brightly lit. A thug on security patrol began eyeing him suspiciously as Kevin shifted uncomfortably from foot to foot. And then all at once the light blinked out, and a bald-headed man in a soiled brown suit hurriedly exited from the booth, mopping his brow. Kevin started forward, his intention being to lull the watchful security thug into believing that he had been waiting for that particular booth to empty all along, but when he glanced anxiously back over his shoulder, he saw that his intimidator had lost all interest in him and was busily distracted in conversation with another man. And by the time Kevin had turned his attention back toward the booth again, the girl inside had exited, too, and was intently lighting a cigarette from the end of another one being proffered by a friend. Neither of them looked even remotely like Vicki.

It was nearly 6:00 AM. Kevin hastily thrust his tokens back in his pocket and headed homeward, in his mind's eye already seated at his kitchen telephone, frantically dialing the hospitals, notifying the police.

She was lying stretched out on the couch when he got there, all alone in the semidarkness, clad only in lacy red panties, her face streaked with tears. "Oh, Kevie!" she gasped gratefully. "I'm so glad you're home!"

And then all at once she was in his arms, her mouth pressed ravenously against his mouth, her yearning body creating a heady suction against his. Kevin grasped her hard against him, slid a hand into her panties, clutched the cheeks of her firm, tight ass. "Oh, Kevie!" she sighed again.

Kevin's senses swam in an inebriating miasma of yearning and lust. He felt strangely at home in his body, and invincible, the way he'd always assumed champion athletes felt when they performed their mind-stunning physical feats. In the bedroom he tore her panties off and rammed in his pulsing ramrod all the way to the root. She came almost instantly, and he'd barely renewed his thrusting when she orgasmed again, much more intensely this time, moaning ecstatically and raking his back with her nails.

Now Kevin knew for certain that Vicki was his woman, that she was the woman he had always been destined to have. When you fucked your woman she lost herself in her desire for you and was brought to climax by the rhythmic movements of your cock inside her, not from three-quarters of an hour of having her labia and her clit licked while delivering a demeaning course of instruction in "Higher! Lower!" and "Damn you, Kevin! When are you ever going to get it right?"

Now Kevin's one, true woman came again, she was screaming when she came again, and Kevin knew that he could make this last forever, that he could make her come fifty, a hundred, a thousand times for him if he wanted her to. And knowing that made him realize that there was no need to make her come a thousand times, no need to assert some puerile mastery over her, no need to prolong this act of lovemaking beyond all reason out of some infantile anxiety that ecstatic moments like these would never come again. What he wanted desperately now was to merge with her if he could, to become one with her if he could, to enter her on a frothing flood tide of semen, to swim inside her like a fish, to wrap himself translucently, protectively, around her egg. He—

"Kevie?"

"Vicki! Darling! I—"

"Tie my hands, Kevie?"

All at once, Kevin became conscious of breathing hard. And although he wasn't certain, exactly, of what he'd just heard, he could feel the tiny maggots of fear excreting their galling acids inside his gut. "Vicki! Darling!" he whispered, leaning down to kiss her lightly on the lips. "I—"

"I want you to tie my wrists, Kevin," she persisted. "I want to have my wrists tied together while you fuck me."

"Vicki, I—"

"I want you to tell me to do things, Kevin. I like it when you tell me things to do."

Kevin took an anxious breath and slowly exhaled it. "I don't want to," he told her.

"Why not?"

Kevin paused.

"You're afraid?" she asked, scrutinizing him.

Kevin blinked silently, striving as best he could to appear relaxed.

"I know why you're afraid. You—"

"I'm not afraid, Vicki," insisted Kevin softly. "I—"

"You're afraid of yourself. Of—"

"Myself?"

"—of what you might—"

"It's just that I'm so close now," he told her, cutting her short with a gentle but nonetheless vehement shake of the head. "It's been so ... so wonderful with you, and if I don't come soon ..."

"Then you'll do it for me next time?" she inquired skeptically.

"Next time, yes," he nodded gratefully, "of course," and began stirring inside her again, his eyes closed, rocking gently back and forth, praying to get hard again. Coming was all that mattered now, unleashing his wad and getting it over with. He focused fleetingly on Nan, sweet Nan, with all her uncounted zillions of rats, and then he remembered Octavia, Octavia of the full, moist lips and the magic-suction mouth. The very thought of her was making him hard again. Octavia would be there for him now that he needed her. When it came to getting his rocks off, Octavia had never failed him.

Nor did she fail him this time. In his mind's eye he let her soft, massaging lips bring him to the very brink of climax—and then he hurriedly withdrew his cock from her mouth in the nick of time and spurted his glistening pearly semen all over her.

CHAPTER 31

▼

It was a glorious spring day at the cemetery, the noon sun shining magnificently overhead, robin redbreasts chirping in the trees then swooping lightly from their branches to gorge themselves on earthworms crawling and undulating out of the ground after nourishing themselves on the decaying remains of the dead.

Kevin could not recall ever having seen the traditional unveiling of a headstone portrayed in a comic book, but he'd seen plenty of funerals, the pulp-paper sky portentous and black with storm clouds, the mourners huddled dankly beneath brooding black umbrellas, the ends of their overcoats lashed by rain and clutched at by the chill fingers of an autumnal wind. It bore hardly any resemblance to the scene prevailing here, at the modest Temple of Zion Cemetery, in Woodlawn, Queens, where barely a blink of an eye ago, it seemed, they had buried his father and where they would bury his mother when her time came. Here the sun was a beaming happy-face in a fingerpaint-blue sky, bouquets of fresh flowers bloomed radiantly at every gravesite, and a carpet of blue-green grass as flawless as Astroturf sprouted reverentially over the honeycombed domain of the dead.

At the head of Kevin's father's grave stood the new marble headstone, still enshrouded in the olive-drab tarpaulin that would continue to cover it—like the sightless hood of a hanged man—until the climactic moment the rabbi pulled the cord to unveil it after intoning a short eulogy and a final prayer. The tarpaulin reminded Kevin of the aged canvas khaki knapsack with leather straps that his father had bought for mountaineering in his youth, and stored for decades in an old foot locker, but never used.

The rabbi's voice droned on in the sanctimonious monotone of a man who has remained unaffected by countless deaths, while Kevin's mother stared clear-eyed in front of her, serene but for the unaccustomed tautness of her jawline, and the tiny clot of relatives bowed their heads reverently, one or another of them now and then shifting their weight restlessly from foot to foot.

Kevin had written a story once about a graveyard of the future, where the arrival of visiting mourners would automatically activate a computer-generated moving, talking hologram of their departed loved one. In the story, Kevin's protagonist, having made a pilgrimage to his father graveside at a time of intense spiritual crisis, had sat hunched with torment on a cold stone bench there, his face buried in his hands, silently pleading with his deceased parent for understanding and guidance, while the idiotic preprogrammed hologram strolled congenially about the grave, gesticulating amiably and mechanically delivering itself of a rash of vacuous parental platitudes that made up the only speech it had.

What was this godlike power his father possessed to inflict involuntary vows of silence on those who loved him, not merely while he lived, but now, all these many months after his death? How, why—for what earthly, unfathomable purpose—had he cast his stifling shroud of silence not merely around Kevin's childhood, but all these years later, from beyond the grave? What manner of ineffable, eldritch malevolence had enabled him to throttle Kevin into dumbness with his paralyzing writer's block? And why, last of all, despite all he now felt, despite all he now knew, couldn't he summon forth the vitriol within himself to hate his father for what he had done to him?

The spirit mask was gone when he got home, the brick wall where it had hung a blank, red stare, the bathroom door shut tight, a kind of furtive rustling emanating from within.

"Vicki?"

Silence. More rustling. Kevin's mind flashed on Nan's teeming rat-world. Skritch skritch! Skritch skritch!

"That's you, right, Vicki?" His hand encircled the metal doorknob in a stealthy embrace. He could tell the door was closed but not locked. "Vicki, are you—"

"Kevin, baby?" returned the plaintive voice within. "Couldn't you—"

Much more abruptly than he'd intended, the door swung open. She was perspiring profusely, and her pupils were like dull blue patches of slate. A double strand of surgical tubing—

"Could you get me a belt or something, Kevin? This effing tubing—"

—was wreathed limply about her left forearm with the yellowy pallor of drowned worms. And the hypodermic syringe—

"—has busted on me, okay, Kevie?"

Kevin raced to the bedroom, frenziedly flung open the closet door. On the chromium tie rack inside it reposed a half-dozen old neckties, a maroon woolen bathrobe sash, and a narrow machine-tooled leather belt that bore a decoratively beaded inscription proclaiming I LOVE MIAMI BEACH!

I love Miami Beach? Good god! ruminated Kevin wordlessly, snatching it off the rack. Where in god's name did I—

A fragile thread on the belt had broken and tiny plastic beads were raining like plastic drizzle onto the floor. Kevin tried to follow which way they were rolling, but visions of gleaming hypodermic needles jabbed at his eyes. He had never been to Miami Beach. He couldn't recall, for the life of him, where that stupid belt had come from. Savage needles of pain stabbed remorselessly at his eyeballs. He couldn't write anymore anyway, what difference would it make if he couldn't see? The drizzling beads blazed a trail to the bathroom like Hansel and Gretel. The wicked witch tried to bake Hansel and Gretel into ginger-bread, but they shoved the witch into the oven instead. Kevin thrust the belt at her and she grabbed it, winding it in a deft, voracious blur about her arm like the constricting coils of a rainbow snake. A wan blue vein bobbed to the surface like a faintly developing photograph, a famished reptile coaxed forth from its torpid, solitary hibernation by the tightening, reassuring embrace of its mate. Then Vicki impaled it, and Kevin emitted a high-pitched, doleful keening sound, like a girl.

"It's not what you think, Kevin," she said to him, her tone of voice poised ambiguously between appeasement and attack.

Kevin blinked at her, like a bird.

"I-I used to have a problem, right? But not anymore."

The spent hypodermic lolled in the sink, its milky translucence frothed by an ebb tide of blood.

"It's just medicine—something the doctor gave me to keep me straight."

"The mask in the living room," he asked her. "Where—"

"Sold it," she snapped flatly, "what'd you think?"

Kevin shut his eyes tightly, his mind all at once unnaturally lucid, his thoughts uncannily clear. Above all else, he had to be careful not to provoke her, lest she suddenly seize the hypodermic and plunge the needle into his heart.

"It hated me from the moment I got here—and you knew it! If you'd so much as given a shit about me, you'd have taken it down!"

Kevin pondered the point abstractedly. Was she right? he wondered. Should he have taken it down? And what if he had?—the thing was huge—where on earth would he have put it?

"Serena had it right on! You never gave a fucking shit—"

She'd risen from her seat on the toilet now, and Kevin was backing fearfully out of the bathroom to get out of her way. She had a puffball of cotton—

"—but that's okay, because I never gave a fucking shit about *you!* You want to know what I thought? I thought—"

She was safely out of the bathroom now, away from the needle. But there were steak knives in the kitchen, and Kevin suddenly became terrified that she might be carrying a gun in her purse.

"—fucking weirdos and zippos—you know what I'm sayin' to you, right?—like I already got saliva drooling on the glass at me all night in the booth! And he lives like a *slob* and he can barely get it up to shoot his load half the time and I'm asking myself is it really *girls* this fucking asshole gets his rocks off on or *what?!* But still—"

She made an abrupt exclamatory gesture, and the cotton puff lodged in the crook of her left arm came loose and fell to the floor.

"—the movie, and I think to myself, So what if it's a stupid shitty fucking movie? So what if he lives like a fucking slob? His name's on it, isn't it? Maybe—"

It was tinged with her blood.

"—he's rich. Or at least a whole fucking lot richer than I'll ever be, right? So—"

She had stalked furiously past him toward the bedroom, gesticulating wildly, all but ignoring him. Maybe she wasn't going to hurt him. Maybe all she was planning to do was go into the bedroom and pack. The cotton ball lay festering on the floor like an open—

"—friends, Hollywood contacts, *something* for christ's sake! But *no!* I had it right the fucking *first* time! You—"

Kevin snatched a tissue from the box on the coffee table, smothered the puffball, ran to the bathroom door and flung it in the toilet bowl. No point in rattling her by making noise now—he could flush it safely away after she was gone. And Lysol—

"—fucking weirdo pervert asshole! Kevin? Are you—"

Once she'd left, he'd soak every inch of the bathroom, sanitize the spot on the living-room floor where the cotton ball fell.

"—listening to me, dammit, Kevin?"

"Yes," he called out diffidently.

She was inside the bedroom now, flinging belongings into the overnight bag. Panties. Cosmetics. Just the things one needed, mused

Kevin sarcastically, for an extended trip. Eugènie had had a set of wheels for her luggage. Maybe that's what Vicki needed—a set of wheels. Maybe what Kevin's apartment needed was a revolving door.

Then Kevin heard the twin latches of the overnight case clack shut.

"… me this time, Kevin! I'm not interested!"

"What!?" he stammered.

"FUCK YOU, KEVIN!" she shrieked at him. "JUST FUCK YOU!" But all at once she seemed haggard and pathetic.

As she strode to the door, she shot a hostile glance down at the spot where the cotton puffball had fallen. "You've picked it up already," she cried, "haven't you, you bastard?"

"Yes," nodded Kevin contritely. .

"FUCK YOU, KEVIN!" she screamed again. "JUST—JUST FUCK YOU!"

He was sure she would slam the door, but by the time she got there she was too tired to slam it. Instead all she did was walk out slowly and let it swing back quietly on its own. Slamming doors all the time must require lots of energy, he thought.

After she was gone he fell asleep in his clothes and didn't wake up till the middle of the following day. Even before eating breakfast, he walked to the hardware store and hired the man there to come home with him and change the locks on his door.

CHAPTER 32

▼

A night at the Catacomb was strictly the Frenchman's idea. "Where you made your mistake, Kevin," he was saying, as they forked over their exorbitant thirty-dollars-per-person admission and threaded their way down the rusty iron spiral staircase to the cavernous sub-basement below, "was in seeing the barrier separating you as an *obstacle* to your relationship instead of as an enhancement and intensification *of* it."

"You're talking about the booth?" Kevin asked him.

"Ah, but of course," returned the Frenchman, with an exasperated sigh. "That booth you have described to me was like a monk's cell, like a confessional, sanctifying and transfiguring all that transpired there. In the booth, you shared with her an encompassing spiritual dimension which imbued the carnal aspect with significance and meaning—a significance and meaning that became lost forever once the intervening obstacle between you had been torn down."

Kevin knew he would be enjoying this discussion a whole lot more if only Jean-Claude Allande didn't look so much like Vicki, with his pale, sensitive face and his head of curly, closely cropped angel hair peroxided the exact same color as hers was, the only immediately striking difference being that his had been liberally splashed with some sort of sparkly-glitzy red hair gel, so that it looked as though it had been sprinkled with vermilion stars. Plus he was clothed neck to toe in garments of soft, supple black leather, giving him the marginally disconcerting appearance of a walking, talking skintight kid glove.

The Catacomb's sub-basement had been renovated to resemble a large cave, or series of interconnecting caves, all of them brooding, dank, almost imperceptibly lit, with simulated black limestone stalactites depending from high-vaulted ceilings and thin streams of ersatz underground runoff tricking steadily down roughly textured rocklike plaster-of-paris walls. Kevin ducked through the low mildewed archway at the base of the staircase and entered the crepuscular subterranean main chamber, half-expecting to be assaulted by a screeching horde of vampire bats of the kind that swarmed and roosted in the deathly secret bat-cavern sanctum of Thurman Cuyler, the renowned billionaire astrophysicist and soldier of fortune who was secretly the dreaded Black Bat.

Here, however, in the darksome depths of the Catacomb, there were no bats, no banks of supercomputers, no mammoth radio telescope tracking the glimmering orbits of countless uncharted stars. Instead, there were anorexic barmaids in calf-length black patent-leather skirts, braless, with fishnet tops, serving up drinks in tall frosted glasses around an oval bar, while the club's patrons, clad in the black leather and metal-studded raiment of bondage and discipline, roved vacantly through the windowless gloom like haggard émigrés from the anonymous personal ads in the S & M magazines. One paunchy middle-aged man, poignantly nude except for a spiked dog collar, hard black rubber cock ring, and leather manacles connected by a length of chrome-plated chain, cringingly circumnavigated the bar once, then nervously switched direction and circumnavigated it again, his head cocked anxiously to one side, his wide eyes darting and fearful, as he searched frantically for his master amid the gloom and din.

Kevin and his French companion ambled casually past the bar, past a set of Puritan-era stocks and a whipping horse, past a life-size guillotine splashed with imitation blood and a pair of bare-bosomed dominatrices in tight black leather dresses and glinting spike-heeled shoes fitfully cracking their cat-o'-nine-tails at nothing in particular while they waited peevishly for willing patrons eager to volunteer themselves for humiliation and abuse.

In a dimly lit antechamber adjacent to the main one, a black girl with purple aureoles the size of flattened tennis balls and skin the color of coffee ice cream, nude save for a pair of lavender-tinted sunglasses adorned with a pair of plastic flamingoes, danced with erotic abandon on a small raised stage, now and then abating her rhythm to allow the fawning tongues of onlookers to probe her vagina while their groping hands caressed the ivory slope of her thighs. One randy patron clambered up onto her platform and, brandishing a mammoth erection in one hand, clutched awkwardly at her bosom and was actually endeavoring to mount her from behind, when suddenly she lurched into some wilder, infinitely more erotic rhythm and whirled sensuously away from him, leaving Kevin to momentarily ponder the enigma of whether she was a Catacomb customer or an employee—for the bizarre milieu in which he now found himself, he'd been told, was one in which life and fantasy were inextricably, if ambiguously, fused, so much so that it was all but impossible to distinguish between the scenarios theatrically staged by the management and those freely and spontaneously enacted by the paying guests.

Allande, meanwhile, despite his having specifically selected this place for them to spend their time together, appeared all but completely indifferent to his surroundings, as though the Catacomb were merely an environment where he knew he could feel at ease, much as a more conventional person might opt for a leisurely stroll through Central Park. The Frenchman droned on, in his intense yet gentle way, about how what he termed "willful disengagement," passivity, was the loftiest mode of human expression and the indispensable foundation of all art. Periodically, he lifted his Vicks sinus inhaler up to his nostrils and imbibed a heady waft of cocaine.

"Ah, but you see, my friend," he was saying, in response to a question Kevin had put to him about Octavia, as they departed the antechamber and resumed their unhurried walk around the premises, "I have fucked Octavia perhaps only two or three times, and even on those times my motive was not mainly sexual, but rather to help her achieve a transition—"

"Transition?" interrupted Kevin.

"Yes," replied Allande, "for the purpose of enabling her to pass comfortably from the initial, material phase of our relationship into the more rarefied, infinitely more rewarding dimensions beyond."

"Meaning?"

"I am a man who adores women, Kevin, who is continually invigorated and renewed by their presence. I derive endless fascination from watching while they eat, or dress, or apply their makeup, or engage themselves in any of the myriad and infinite details of their lives. That is why I live with *two* women, because—"

"Yes?"

"—so that I can immerse myself in, scrutinize, how they are when they are alone, and then, how they are when they are with one another. For me, it is like being alone in a great, solitary cathedral—with god!"

"And Octavia?" inquired Kevin uncertainly.

The Frenchman gave an embarrassed, self-deprecating shrug. "I have not succeeded to make it plain to you, have I?" he sighed. "Perhaps my English—"

"Your English is fine," retorted Kevin, a bit irritably. "It's just—"

"I watch the women, do you see, Kevin? I watch them eating, fucking, shitting. Everything meaningful in my life comes to me from that. Everything else—my art, everything—is nothing but a piece of shit. By watching, I merge with them, I partake of them, in some meager, unworthy way I become them—even if it is only mainly a delusion. In the beginning, when Octavia would come, I would fuck her. But it is something I would do for her benefit only, to put her at her ease, to give her, in my own way, the kind of gratification that I know she has grown accustomed to receiving from men. But my own gratifications come from the next phase, the higher phase, the phase of being able to lie back in our bed and watch while she makes passionate love with Françoise and Helène, and imagine that I am one, two, even all three of us at once." He paused a moment, then added, "The life's goal of every true artist, Kevin, is to annihilate the man he has been born as in order to be able to surrender his soul to the woman inside himself yearning to breathe free."

By now their stroll had brought them to another dark alcove, where a clot of onlookers, male and female, had formed a silent voyeuristic circle around an attractive young woman in bluejeans and polka-dot blouse administering a harsh spanking with an assortment of variously shaped wooden paddles to a slightly older man who knelt obediently over a low bench, his button-down shirt gathered up under his armpits, his corduroy slacks and boxer shorts bunched down together around his calves.

The woman whaled unmercifully away at his buttocks, which were red and raw from the pounding, while he stoically bit his lip and endured the thrashing, crying out only occasionally whenever an especially hard blow was struck. Periodically her arm would tire, or he would go too long without whimpering, and this would prompt her to pause a moment to exchange whatever paddle she was currently using for one that was heavier.

Kevin and Allande had been watching the spanking for what seemed like some time when Kevin suddenly realized that he was about to throw up. Elbowing his way out of the crowded alcove as swiftly and undisruptively as possible, he scurried hurriedly back to the oval bar, cast desperately about for the men's room, padded quickly inside it and hook-latched the door—even as his undulating waves of nausea mysteriously began to subside.

Kevin sat down on the toilet seat lid and took a few slow deep breaths. The room was a tiny one, scarcely larger than Vicki's booth, with nothing but the toilet bowl, a hot-air blower for drying one's hands, and an ancient sink. Kevin stared deeply into the cracked mirror above it, and, for a fleeting instant, fantasized that he was peering through the transparent plexiglass wall panel of his booth into the adjoining booth, Vicki's booth, and that the image he saw peering back at him was her image looking out at him from the depths of a faraway world.

He turned on the cold-water tap, cupped his hands, and splashed a half-dozen handfuls of cold water onto his face. The water trickled out slowly, and Kevin had to wait forever for his cupped hands to fill up, but he waited. Finally, he turned off the faucet and looked around for a towel, but there was none, only the hot-air blower. Kevin used it to dry his hands and then walked back out into the Catacomb with his face still sopping wet.

He cast about for Allande, but couldn't find him. The spanking crowd had evidently called it quits, and except for the paddles the alcove was empty. Kevin shambled to the bar and treated himself to a tepid five-dollar Coke. The hard nipples of the emaciated barmaid who served it protruded unappetizingly through her fishnet top, like snails, but the Coke syrup served to allay his still-lingering nausea.

It was the low moan he heard wafting through the crepuscular dimness that jolted him back to reality and made his stomach start churning all over again. Hoisting himself from his barstool and craning his neck for a better view over the heads of a swiftly gathering throng, Kevin could just make out the image of Jean-Claude Allande pinioned to the whipping horse, his leather shirt stripped open, his eyes glazed in pain and ecstasy as the twin dominatrices mercilessly lashed him with their whips. A pair of gleaming golden posts, much like the kind women wore in pierced ears, had been thrust through his nipples, and a solitary diamond glistened at the end of each post, like a star.

CHAPTER 33

▼

"Trouble, Kev."

"Guido?"

It was nearly 5:00 AM, and Kevin had just barely gotten home from the Catacomb when the telephone rang.

"Jesus fucking Christ, Guido! Do you know what—"

"Yeah, I know, Kev. I'm sorry. But I figured I oughtta clue you in before—"

Kevin had wrenched open the front door and lunged frantically for the receiver, reasoning that only Vicki could possibly be calling him at 5:00 AM. The as-yet-uncollected remnants of her possessions—clothing, toiletries, a forgotten suitcase—still trailed hauntingly about his apartment like a cavalcade of ghosts. In recent days, there had been two or three odd hang-ups on his answering machine. He'd suspected, no, hoped—

"—the shit hits the fuckin' fan."

"What was that again, Guido?" Kevin asked.

"Wake up and sniff the fuckin' java, will you, Kevin? It's five o'clock in the fuckin' morning, for christ's sake! I been tryin' to get through to you all—"

"Okay, Guido. I'm sorry. Go ahead. What's—"

"It's about the loans, Kev. I—"

"The loans? Good lord! You mean you won't be able to keep lend—"

"I'm in a jam, Kevin—what you call a squeeze. I was holdin' a little paper—you get me?—and I hadda let it all go."

"Go? What go?!"

"I hadda lay off my paper, Kevin, all of it. Not—"

"Guido, I'm sorry, but I still don't—"

"For christ's sake, Kevin! You don't understand English? All them dead presidents I been fronting you—so what the hell am I, a savings and loan? And they ain't makin' out so good these days either, by the way. So—"

"So?"

"—I got stretched thinsies a little bit, that's all. For a while there it looked like the bottom was gonna fall out. So I didn't have no fuckin' choice. It was either lay off the paper—right?—or be in a world of shit. So I took a coupla outstanding notes I had—yours, one or two others—and I sold 'em off for about a quarter on the dollar or whatever measly chickenshit I could—"

"You mean you sold my loans?" gasped Kevin. "You mean now I owe the money to—someone else!?"

"You got it."

"WHO?!"

"There's not that many people around actually buys this kinda horseshit, Kevin. I mean you know me—I hate to tell tales outa school. But—"

"*WHO??*"

"The hard guys, Kevin. That's—"

"Oh my god! You mean—gangsters?!?"

"Aw, c'mon, Kevin, please! Let's have a little tact and diplomacy, okay? All it—"

"Spare me the small talk, Guido. When do I have to start paying it back?"

"Friday."

"Friday? Why, that's the—"

"Day after tomorrow. Right. So what the hell? You got forty—"

"How much?"

"What, Kevin?"

"How much are they going to want from me on Friday?"

"Oh, that's easy. All of it. And in cash. Wait a sec. I got—"

"*ALL?!?*"

"—the numbers, figures, right here. Yeah, okay, here it is. Altogether, in round numbers, it comes out to—"

"Dammit, Guido, this is—"

"—thirty-four thousand eight hundred sixty dollars—"

"That's insane! I barely borrowed half—"

"—including interest."

"Interest? Fuck you, interest! You said—"

"I said three months. And I been golden, you know that, even though it coulda got me in lotsa trouble. So keep in touch—don't be a stranger. And tell you what—next time you're up at Dynamic, what say I take you out for a beer?" Pause. "Oh, wait a minute. I forgot. You don't even drink beer. Better make that a Coke."

And he hung up.

Kevin quietly set down the receiver and slumped back on the couch. He couldn't believe how unaccountably calm and clear-headed he felt, with none of the churning anxiety and turmoil that had almost made him puke at the Catacomb. It was almost as though he had been presented with a relatively undemanding math problem—somebody else's math problem—and given forty-eight hours in which to solve it. Two of the credit cards in his wallet were good for cash advances, one with an available credit line of sixty-seven hundred, the other with a limit of five thousand dollars. Over and above that, he had four thousand and change in a money market, squirreled away over the last six months through frugal use of the eighteen thousand he'd borrowed from Gallante. And there he was, by god, already hovering up around the sixteen-thousand-dollar mark, and he hadn't even begun to work up a sweat.

Kevin glanced at his watch—5:37 AM—and ambled into the kitchen for a bite to eat. He discovered an all-but-forgotten box of chocolate-covered marshmallow cookies hiding in the fridge—they'd gotten all hard and gummy the way he liked them—and washed all eight of them down with instant coffee that looked and tasted like mud. The caffeine jolt kicked him into high gear momentarily, but the sugar rush that followed sent him crashing down again. Kevin staggered into his bedroom and was asleep from practically the moment he hit the bed.

By the time he awoke it was late afternoon, too late to get to the bank and borrow the money he needed out of those credit cards. But nestled serenely among his mail that day was a check from Dynamic for twenty-three hundred dollars—a royalty payment on the Shambler trade paperbacks—which Kevin knew he could turn into instant money merely by cashing it the following morning, Thursday, at the bank where Dynamic maintained its account. He spent the remainder of the day and evening closeted with the telephone and his Rolodex, calling up Hinder, Scanlon, Bernstein, and practically everyone else he knew. Everyone he spoke to was gracious and happy to help him. By midnight he'd amassed an additional seven thousand dollars, giving him a total of twenty-five thousand in all. Through it all, he was amazed how lucid and carefree he felt, how benevolent and wonderful the whole world seemed.

And then finally he dialed Jordan Mason, whom he'd consciously and confidently reserved for last. For Mason was indisputably Kevin's most affluent friend, and his generosity, like many other aspects of his life, was legendary. On one justifiably renowned occasion, after the home of some friends of his had been wiped out by a mudslide, Mason had personally replaced its entire contents at his own expense, including a valuable silent movie collection and an antique display case filled with Iroquois masks.

"Hello, Jordan?" exclaimed Kevin expectantly when Mason's receiver finally picked up. "This—"

"Mason here!" shot back the mechanical rejoinder from the far end. "The colossal fucking genius is in deep creative mode right now, so if you're sitting there waiting for the fucking beep to sound, forget it and buzz off. And if it's you, George, you fucking cheapskate, you better believe Friday morning's gonna be your last chance to beat the other couples, so how's about you try to come up with a *real* number this time, and not just another pathetic, sick joke...."

Kevin tried to reach Mason a few more times that night, and then tried again the next day, Thursday, whenever he wasn't racing around town to cash his Dynamic check, close out his money market, and borrow up to the limit on his credit cards. He was less than ten thousand dollars shy of his needed total now, and so certain that Mason would help him that he resisted the temptation to call his mother, both to avoid worrying her and humiliating himself, despite the fact that his continuing inability to reach Mason was beginning to tie a raw knot in his gut. He spent the entire night in the living room, wide awake, with all the cash he'd collected piled in a shopping bag, popping tranquilizers, watching porno tapes, and jerking off like a maniac. At nine o'clock Friday morning, for about the one-millionth time, he dialed Jordan Mason's number again.

"Mason here!" spat the fucking answering machine contemptuously. "The colossal fucking genius is—"

"Okay, George, you asshole!" broke in Mason's real voice suddenly. "So you've gotten me out of the rack at some ungodly fucking hour! I hope—"

"Jordan, it's me!" interjected Kevin hastily. "I'm in a terrible jam, Jordan. I need—"

"Good god! Kevin? Is that—"

"Yes, Jordan. It's—"

"Well what the fuck, Kevin! Spit it out, you nimnod! You sound like shit, you know that, Kevin? You sound like you're up to your rancid ears in a cesspool of squirrel shit!"

Kevin breathlessly gasped out his horror story of Guido Gallante and the huge loans. In his mind's eye he could see Mason scowling at him disapprovingly and shaking his head.

"How much you need?" snapped Mason.

"I've already got most of it," stammered Kevin contritely. "If I just had ten thou—"

"You got it," cut in Mason. "Anything else?"

"Actually, I might not even need exactly the whole ten thousand," ran on Kevin compulsively. "It could be I could get by with—"

"I thought we'd just about wrung this topic dry, Kevin, but if you're not bored with it yet—"

"No, Jordan!" gulped Kevin. "You're right! I—"

The sound of the front doorbell exploded raucously against his eardrums like an electronically intensified hive of bees. He was contemplating ignoring it when it rang again—more insistently this time—and he found himself flashing on that amazing night five months ago when Vicki came to him at one in the morning while he was watching TV.

Kevin excused himself from the phone a minute and raced to the door. The burly giant he practically smacked into when he opened it was clad in a khaki mechanic's jumpsuit and a frankly puerile-looking long-billed cap. Kevin was momentarily bewildered as to how he'd got through the front gate, but sometimes the landlord—

"Yo! Got the beans?" growled the man.

"What?!" asked Kevin.

"Dis ain't trick or treat, asshole!" rumbled the giant khaki mechanic. "You got them thirty-five donkeys all wrapped up or what?"

"Guido!" stammered Kevin bewilderedly. "Did Guido—"

"Jesus friggin' Christ, you're friggin' stupid," grumbled the mechanic irritably, shoving Kevin violently through his open doorway onto the living-room floor. "You really think this is some fuckin' radio show, don'tcha? Now, you got the balloons you owe us, or—"

"The bag! The … the shopping bag!" mewled Kevin, and pointed it out with a quavering hand.

The mechanic peered perfunctorily into it. "It's all here, right?" he demanded off-handedly, somehow contriving to make a peculiar sucking sound with his tongue and lips. "'Cause you know time's money, right, guy? It rubs us the wrong way when we gotta make two trips!"

"No!" gasped Kevin. "Not exactly all of it, no! But—"

"Billy goats butt," chortled the mechanic with a kind of amiable malevolence, as he lumbered toward Kevin like a steamroller about to pulverize a clump of dirt. "I bet you've heard that stupid expression so many times you're sick of it, right?"

The rest of it was like one of those strange out-of-body experiences you read about: it's happening to you, all right, but somehow it's as if you're not really there.

CHAPTER 34

▼

"... out of here, we'll hop into that spread-lipped old whore that Freddy lavishes so much unrequited devotion on, and we'll head up the ..."

Good old Dynamic. At least they hadn't cut off his hospitalization coverage. It was bad enough that he looked like Boris Karloff in *The Return of the Mummy* without his having to face the scary prospect of a ten-thousand-dollar hospital bill he'd have no way to pay. He ruminated fleetingly on the unsettling notion of hospitals turning over their delinquent accounts to the "hard guys," pondering whether there might not be some sort of story in it, and then just as quickly discarded the idea, having concluded that the whole scenario just wasn't flashy enough for comic books. And then he flashed on Vicki, and he wished—

"... anything I've been telling you, Kevin?"

—he wished to god it was Vicki sitting here by his bedside and not nerdy Sol Bernstein.

"Dammit, Kevin! Have you—"

"Sure," replied Kevin gently. "I'm sorry, Solly."

"It's like a once-in-a-lifetime opportunity!" burbled Bernstein ecstatically. "Think of it! It's got everything! Sex, mystery, the glories of nature! And it'll be good for you, Kevin, I mean that—help you take

your mind off your...." His voice trailed off hopelessly, as his bespecta-
cled eyes roved glumly over the supine Kevin, swathed head to toe in
bandages and plaster casts. "Off your broken—"

"Everything," grinned Kevin impishly, the way his father used to,
and Bernstein laughed.

"It's not every day something extraordinary like this happens,
Kevin!" continued Bernstein eagerly. "I mean this definitely qualifies as
some kind of major fucking event, am I right? To have ac—"

"How?" interrupted Kevin suddenly, all at once irked by his visitor's
adolescent enthusiasm.

"How?" repeated Bernstein vacuously. "You mean how—"

"Did you find her?"

"You mean after all this time? After all these years?"

"Solly, look," interjected Kevin impatiently, raising himself up to
lean on his arms, for the time being his only two functional limbs. "If
it's that you want to keep it a goddam secret or something, just—"

"A private detective," blurted Bernstein.

"What?"

"A detective agency. Minsk and I chipped in. They found her in two
days, in New Hampshire, in a town called—"

"But didn't that kind of take the challenge out of it, Solly? I mean
the—"

"Yeah, kind of," winced Bernstein sheepishly. "But she was really
nice to me when I called her, Kevin, I mean it. I mean I felt kind of
ratty and all, about hiring the detective and everything. Like she's an
old woman now, you know? I guess she's entitled to her privacy. But I
called her up, and I made myself swear that if she gave me any resis-
tance, or—or anything, I'd just throw away her address and phone
number and never, ever disclose it to anyone and just forget the whole
thing. But I just told her who I was and everything, and about my collection, and about how a bunch of us are lifelong fans of hers, and
how—"

"And what did she have to say then?"

"She was really great, Kevin. I mean it. She was this great, warm, friendly old lady, like she was my grandmother or something. So of course I got brave, and I asked her if a few of us could maybe, well, visit her and just kind of more or less pay our respects to her and—"

"And so she said …?"

"She said yes, Kevin. So we're going—you, me, Scanlon, and Freddy. We're going in that old antique slut of a convertible that old Freddy lavishes more love and attention on than he does his wife. I just hope—"

"Hope?"

"I just hope seeing you all embalmed like this doesn't give her a minor-league heart attack! I mean, you will be able to hobble around on crutches by then, won't you, Kevin?"

CHAPTER 35

▼

The old farmhouse in Center Ossipee bustled with life. Three young children and a shaggy dog roughhoused in the front yard, four more kids played blindman's buff inside the house, and everywhere Kevin looked he spied a puppy or a cat.

"My grandchildren," beamed Vera Hale Durning, and graciously ushered them inside, through the country kitchen and the dining area, past the wood-burning stove, into the pleasantly furnished sunlit main room beyond. Their hostess was in her early sixties, a gracefully aging, wholly unglamorous rural wife and homemaker, but there was no doubt at all who she was, no doubt whatsoever that she was the bona fide late-middle-aged incarnation of the nubile young bondage queen whose ingenuously vulnerable brown eyes and suggestively sensuous mouth smiled provocatively yet imploringly out at you from the ring-bound oversized plastic sleeves of Bernstein's bulging portfolios of vintage World War II-era magazine clippings and girlie-calendar art.

"How many grandchildren do you have?" inquired Freddy Minsk casually, easing himself down comfortably into a rumpled cloth-covered armchair while at the same time casting a vigilant glance out the window to assure himself that no larcenous locals harbored felonious designs on his classic 1957 Chevy Bel Air parked in the driveway outside.

"It's an even dozen now," smiled Mrs. Durning. "Not so awfully many, really, when you have eight grown-up children."

"Eight?!" gasped Solly Bernstein, barely able to conceal his abject horror, as he leaned back lazily on the flower-print sofa, clutching the single overstuffed portfolio of choice Vera Hale memorabilia he'd brought up here with him.

"Walter and I were both married before," explained Mrs. Durning. "Four of them were his, two were mine, and we had two together, a boy and a girl. On Sundays like this, especially when Walter isn't slaving away at his coal forge, we like nothing better than to have them over."

"Coal forge?" asked Kevin.. "You mean he's a metalsmith?"

"Walter makes wonderful things," she affirmed with a nod. "Don't worry, I'll be sure and have him give you the whole cook's tour while you're here."

Ed Scanlon cleared his throat. It had been a lengthy five-and-a-half-hour drive from New York, and all he'd had to keep his bodily organs from drying up completely was one lone six-pack of beer.

"Can I get you fellows some refreshments?" Mrs. Durning inquired. "Dinner won't be ready for a while yet, but—"

"A beer would be great!" exclaimed Scanlon.

"Beers all around, then?" offered their hostess.

"Do you maybe have a soft drink?" asked Bernstein. "The three of us—"

"Of course I do," she answered, starting for the kitchen. "And with all these kids around, we've probably got just about any flavor you'd like."

*   *   *   *

"What I don't think I understand," she continued, after returning minutes later with a tray of drinks and a platter of crackers and two types of cheese, "is why you gentlemen went to all this trouble to learn my whereabouts and drive all the way up here from New York to see me."

Kevin shifted his gaze back and forth between Minsk and Bernstein, who were exchanging mildly apprehensive glances, while Scanlon, who may as well have been on Mars, stared blankly up at the ceiling, ignoring his glass and nonchalantly chugalugging his beer from the can.

"Well, you see," began Bernstein awkwardly, "it's like, well, we're your *fans!*"

"Why, that's very flattering," she replied. "I didn't know I *had* fans."

"But you *do!*" exclaimed Bernstein breathlessly. "Of course you do! *Scads* of them! We—"

"Sol here is really your greatest admirer," cut in Minsk. "He's—"

"Yeah, rabid," mumbled Scanlon sarcastically, crumpling the empty beer can in his oversized hands and letting it fall with a portentous clunk back down onto the tray.

"He adores you!" persisted Minsk. "And so do—"

"Laying it on a little thick, aren't you, Minsk?" growled Scanlon, evidently grown a lot tipsier—and nastier—from downing that one six-pack than Kevin ever would have supposed. "When the hell did you ever—"

"It's like a hobby, Mrs. Durning," interjected Kevin with diplomatic haste. "Or a cult. Maybe more like a cult."

"A cult?" she inquired curiously, her irises widening.

"Yes, ma'am," answered Kevin. "You see, all four of us here are in the comic book—I mean, like for example, have you ever heard of Power Man?"

"You mean the comics hero?"

"Well, then," Kevin nodded, "you know how, in his secret identity, he's a schoolteacher. I mean, these days they're putting him through a lot of changes and sending him to law school at night and, well, kind of reinventing him to become some kind of big-wheel defense attorney and maybe get into politics, but most people still remember him as what he always used to be, a schoolteacher."

"Yes?"

"And you remember when they had that Power Man TV show in the Fifties, and there was another teacher in the school who liked him in his schoolteacher identity but who thought Power Man was arrogant and conceited, but he was always rejecting her advances because he always felt it would be dangerous to involve her in his life so long as he was out there being Power Man? Remember that? Well, there was an obscure actress who played that role and who practically never became known for anything else, and who dropped out of sight when the show was canceled and may as well have died after that, except that she didn't die, and now there are people, really dedicated Power Man fans—"

"We call 'em 'heavy breathers,'" grumped Ed Scanlon sardonically, slowly sweeping the ceiling with the whites of his eyes.

"—who are just obsessed and fascinated with everything there is to know about Power Man, and his stories, and the toys and wristwatches and the cereal premiums, and the movie serials from the Forties, and that TV show, and all the actors who—"

"You're putting her to sleep, Kevin," growled Scanlon intolerantly.

"No, that's not true," contradicted Mrs. Durning gently. "I'm interested. Fascinated. Go on, please, Kevin."

"Well, that's about it," shrugged Kevin. "For a long time, no one even knew where Alicia Maynard was, or even whether she was still alive. And then some fans found her, and there was a huge comics convention in San Diego, and they flew her in, and she autographed old publicity stills and lobby cards and gave a talk on what it was like to be in that series and how she felt years afterward when she saw those TV shots of Alan Bolland, who'd played Power Man all those years, being decapitated by that helicopter rotor during that—anyway, all I mean is, millions of people adored that show, and still adore it, and finding out where she was after all those years was like an adventure, and terrifically exciting for the people who found her and went to see her and finally brought her forward to meet her fans and kind of bask in the

glow of the way they felt about her and see her at long last get some of
the recognition she deserved."

"It's a kind of nostalgia, then," commented Mrs. Durning thoughtfully.

"Yes," replied Kevin, "that's right. Except we were barely infants
when that TV series ran, and a lot of Alicia Maynard's major fans
weren't even *alive* when—"

"Nostalgia for a past you never even knew," mused their hostess
aloud. "A past you were never even a part of."

"Hey, come on, you guys!" pleaded Kevin. "Don't make me carry
the ball all alone like this. Help me out here. Show her, Solly. Show her
all that wonderful stuff you've—"

"Yeah, Solly!" jibed Scanlon caustically. "And while you're at it, why
not tell her how much you've *paid* for—"

"It's become awfully rare, Mrs. Durning," explained Freddy. "I
mean, like with comic books, and old toys, and baseball cards, there's a
regular market you can go to, and dealers, and even price guides to tell
you what the current prices are. But with your stuff—"

"It's like a super-highly-specialized underground," proclaimed Bernstein proudly. "Like what Kevin said before, a cult, even though that
wouldn't be my favorite word for it. It's taken me years just to"—he
bumblingly thrust some of his calendars and photos at her—"years just
to—"

"We've been searching for you for years!" sighed Freddy Minsk reverently. "You may not believe this, but this is one of the most meaningful—"

"There's a joke around the industry," cracked Scanlon sardonically,
"that if Minsk and Bernstein ever actually found you, they'd have no
alternative left but to jump—"

"You've been such an inspiration to us," whispered Solly softly.

"Inspiration?" queried Mrs. Durning incredulously, leafing casually
through the material Bernstein had handed her.

"You see, most of us are artists," Freddy explained. "And in comics, the figures, the men and the women, are kind of idealized, you know what I mean? It's all got to be lifelike, but it's not so much realistic as it is idealized, perfect, a world of wonder. So the heroes, like Kevin was telling you about Power Man, all have really perfect physiques, like with maybe the kind of body you always wished you had when you were an ugly, scrawny little kid. No one really has a build like that, even the ratio of head size to body length is changed, altered, to create this kind of ideal we're talking about. And the women—"

"The women are the women of our dreams," interjected Kevin wistfully. "Like those trapeze artists and bareback riders in the circus when you were a kid, who always—"

"We're always looking through magazines and stuff," Freddy Minsk went on, "always searching for great models we can use. We found some of your old bondage spreads five or six years ago and we were hooked. See?" he exclaimed, hastily snatching a sheaf of comic book drawings from his own portfolio, "Look! These are some pages I drew for a limited series called *The Spectral Avenger*! See the one with the huge bird wings over here? That's you! And that's you over here! And there too! I mean, the costume is all superheroine horseshit! But the face, the eyes—and see?—all these other girls in here are porno stars too! Look! There's—"

Kevin readjusted his crutches against the edge of the sofa—and wished to god that Minsk had been able to come up with some more euphemistic phrase than "porno stars" to—

"—Tracie Camden and Kitten Délicieuse and—"

"Porno stars? For children?" objected Mrs. Durning gently.

Minsk and Bernstein shot each other hurried, apprehensive looks. "No one knows where they come from but us," Minsk assured her solemnly. "I swear, it's our secret."

Mrs. Durning smiled at them indulgently. She really was being awfully tolerant of them, Kevin thought.

"Well, I'm flattered," she said finally, matter-of-factly. "You've clearly gone to so much trouble, but—what is it exactly you'd like me to do for you?"

"Well, we'd like to interview you," replied Bernstein. "You know, ask you some questions."

"All right," shrugged Mrs. Durning self-effacingly. "Ask away."

"Well, for starters," began Bernstein earnestly, "how did you get into it?"

Pause. "Into it?" she asked him perplexedly.

"Well, um, let's maybe start with this pinup stuff," replied Bernstein, clearing his throat. "Like this calendar you did for Pyramid Auto Parts. It's the earliest thing I've ever found of yours. Was it the first—"

"Yes," she replied, "it was, at least as—"

"Tell us how it happened," prodded Bernstein.

"Happened?"

"Yeah, well, like did they approach you, and ask you, or did you just know they had an annual calendar, so you—"

"No," she answered. "I had a boyfriend there, a mechanic. He asked me if I'd—"

"And you agreed."

"Yes."

"Did they pay you?"

"Yes, they did."

"Can you recall how much?"

"Twenty-five dollars."

"Whew! Not much!" commented Bernstein.

"We're talking about nineteen-thirty-seven money here, Solly," interjected Kevin.

"Oh yeah, right. How old were you?" he asked her.

"Fifteen."

"Fifteen! Wow! And this thing for Pyramid was your very first, right?"

"Yes, that's right."

"Were you living at home at the time?"

"Yes."

"With your parents?"

"Yes."

"What'd they think?"

Vera Hale Durning affected a nonchalant shrug.

"Did they know about it?"

"Yes."

"Well, then, what'd they think? Did they—"

"It upset them more than I thought it would, actually. My father—"

"Your father? What'd—"

"You really ought to stop interrupting her, Solly," admonished Kevin.

"No, that's all right, Kevin," she said reassuringly, turning to face him. "But thank you."

"You said your father was pretty upset about it," continued Bernstein.

"Yes," she nodded affirmatively, "he was."

"Well, tell us, what kind of a man was he?"

"Kind?"

"Like, what'd he do for a living?"

"He was an elementary-school principal."

"A school principal?" exclaimed Bernstein. "In an elementary school? I mean unless things were really different then, he must've gone completely—"

"Yes," she smiled, "you're right. We lived in a small town. The calendar caused something of a local uproar. He became very—very upset."

"But you did more of them."

"Yes."

"Lots more. I mean, I have this—"

"Yes, you're right. There was a short pause after the first one, but then I did scores of them."

"Well, maybe you could tell us a little about what your home life was like," asked Bernstein. "I mean, were you a happy kid?"

"No," she answered, pursing her lips thoughtfully, "I don't think so."

"Well, I mean, what was it like at home when you were a kid growing up? I mean, was it a creepshow or—"

"Creepshow?" she asked him.

"Yeah, you know. Like, did he beat you or—"

"No, he—"

"—or abuse you when you were a kid, or—"

"Abuse—yes—he did."

"Good god! You mean incest?!" shrieked Bernstein.

"That's enough, Solly!" interjected Kevin sternly. "You're going too—"

"It's hot as hell in here!" grumbled Ed Scanlon. "Does anybody else know that?"

"It's all right, Kevin," remarked Mrs. Durning, blinking, then shifting her attention back to Bernstein. "Yes, incest," she answered simply. "Often. Repeatedly. For nearly eleven years."

"Oh, Jesus," sighed Freddy Minsk. "Look, Vera. I-I mean Mrs. Durning. Honest, we're—"

"What happened then?" persisted Bernstein.

"Then?"

"Yeah. To your father. Did you ever report him? Was he ever arrested or—"

"He died."

"Of what?"

"A stroke. He started speaking in nonsense syllables at breakfast one morning, and then all at once he just pitched over dead."

"And that was in—"

"April. Nineteen-forty-three."

"Nineteen-forty-three!" cried Bernstein. "Good christ! I mean, excuse me. But wasn't that the year—"

"Yes," nodded Vera Durning, "it was."

"What year we talkin' about, Solly boy?" piped up Scanlon jauntily. "Clue—"

"The year she did her first bondage layout for *Daring Discipline*. Lookit! Issue number four. I-I have it right here! I paid—"

"What made you start doing it *then?*" inquired Minsk suddenly. Was there some—"

"Yeah! And why B & D, for christ's sake?" chimed in Bernstein. "I mean, you were an incredible knockout! Even limiting it to porno, you could've done anything! So why—"

"Were you into kink yourself?" broke in Scanlon. "Was that it? You liked—"

"Never," she answered quietly, shaking her head.

"Then why the hell?" shot back Bernstein.

"Yeah, why?" echoed Freddy Minsk.

"Well," she shrugged, "it did pay pretty well. Not all the girls would do it. It seemed fairly harmless, really, catering to other people's fantasies. And as I've said, the money—"

"Vera? Sugar?" broke in an unfamiliar male voice. "You know I don't mean to—"

The rawboned man framed in the doorway was about seventy, with a thick gray beard and matching soft gray eyes. The sinews rippling in the backs of his hands were like strands of steel cable adroitly manipulating the movements of ten swollen but nimble digital marionettes.

"Don't be silly," answered Vera Durning warmly. "Gentlemen, this is Walter, my husband. Walter, these are those young fellows who called up from—"

"I figured. Nice to meet you boys," he said affably. "You have a good trip up?"

"Great," volunteered Freddy. "It's been a really gorgeous day."

"I've kind of been admiring your old car out there," remarked Walter Durning, raising his right arm to point across the room to the window. "Must be a pain in the neck, though, when you have to find parts."

"It is," replied Freddy respectfully. "The only way is at meets and conventions."

"Conventions?"

"Car shows. Get-togethers of people who own or collect old cars. There are always dealers who—"

"It's like a hobby," chimed in Bernstein. "The idea is to buy some classic old heap and then slowly rebuild it from the ground up using only vintage parts manufactured for that precise model in the exact same month and year as the body."

"Sounds like fun," smiled Walter Durning indulgently.

"Right now I'm looking for a vent window and it's driving me crazy," exclaimed Freddy.

"We'll swap you the whole bucket of worms for four bus tickets home and a six-pack," wisecracked Ed Scanlon drily.

"How are the rose gates coming, Walter?" inquired Mrs. Durning.

"Fine," he answered. "But I think I've wrestled with 'em enough for a Sunday. And besides, those youngsters are starting to get restless for—"

"Dinner!" exclaimed his wife. "Oh my heavens! How's—"

"Don't worry yourself. It's fine," he replied. "I checked it on the way in. Tossed the salad while I was at it, too. Come on, fellas," he added, with a hospitable toss of his head. "You boys are in for a treat!"

*　　*　　*　　*

The pot-roast dinner was delicious, and when the grandchildren found out that Kevin and his friends wrote and drew comic books, they went completely bananas, especially the three boys. Fortunately, Freddy had a big boxful in the car, and they promised that before they left they'd hand them out.

After dinner, they helped clear the table and then trooped out to Walt Durning's workshop to have a look at his work. The workshop building, converted from an old barn, featured a spacious loft filled with sheets, bars, and strips of copper, aluminum, and iron; shelves and wall brackets crammed with swages, fullers, and other metalworking implements; welding equipment and a pair of anvils; and a large coal forge. Various metalworks in progress lay across workbenches or stood propped in wooden racks arrayed along one wall, including a magnificent pair of wrought-iron gates, clearly destined to grace the entranceway to some fabulous estate, gracefully rounded into nuanced arches at the top and adorned with delicate clusters of iron roses so wistful and lifelike in appearance that, except for their black color, they looked certain to wilt with the first fall freeze. Close by it stood an elaborate grille, on which velvet-bodied hummingbirds, their wings seeming to beat in a veritable blur of motion, drained the sweet nectar of orchids, while on a lengthy section of fencing some twelve feet away, powder-winged butterflies cavorted and mated in a glorious wrought-iron spring. When Walter Durning lay one of the rose gates across a trestle and, donning his welder's helmet, ignited his welding torch in order to give his four guests a brief demonstration in metalworking, his helmeted face, eerily lit by the incandescent shower of sparks from the welding torch, became imbued, at least to Kevin's eyes, with a disconcerting ambiguity akin to that aroused by the New Guinea spirit mask—at once male and female, intimidating and beneficent—that Vicki had stolen and sold to pay for her dope.

Kevin slipped away from the demonstration, out of the workshop, and propelled himself by small vaults of his crutches across the fifty yards or so to the house. Vera Durning was placing the last of the just-washed dishes in the drainer when he got there, and he knew this would likely be his only chance to talk with her alone, away from the others.

"Is something wrong, Kevin?" she asked him. "Are you all right?"

"Yes," he answered. "Fine. And you and your husband have been just terrific. And dinner was really delicious. Thanks."

"But?"

Kevin felt as though she were peering into his mind. "But we all owe you an apology, a big one. We had no right to intrude on you like this, no right to ask all those—"

"But you haven't intruded, Kevin. I invited you. Your friend Solly called me, and told me exactly what you were all interested in, and I told him you were all perfectly welcome. Believe me, I'm—"

"Why?" asked Kevin.

"Why did I say you could come?"

"Yes, why?"

She paused a moment, smiled. Kevin watched her blink, luxuriate in a slightly playful shrug. "Why not?"

"We shouldn't have come," mused Kevin only half-aloud. "But, anyway...."

"Yes?"

"It helped me. I don't know how, but I know it did."

She was scrutinizing him gently now, her eyes focused on him empathetically, her lips pursed. "I'm sorry, Kevin, but I don't think I—"

"It helped me because lately I've been dwelling on everything, feeling so sorry for myself, so preoccupied with my own problems. So I hope it's okay to say this, but your story kind of helped me put some things into perspective, made me realize that my problems—"

"You mean your legs?"

"Huh-!?"

"The accident, or whatever it was, in which you broke your legs?"

"You mean these?" laughed Kevin. "Oh, jeez, no. I mean my writing. I'm a writer, but I haven't been able to write a line since the day my father died. It's—"

"When my father died," she began, gently interrupting him, "I felt that it was my fault he'd died, that I was responsible."

"You did?" exclaimed Kevin. "But why, for god's sake? That's—"

"Crazy? Perhaps it was. But deep down I knew that the reason I'd posed for those calendars was to humiliate him, to get back at him for all the unforgivable things he'd done to me. So when he died, when he had that stroke, I felt I'd done it to him, that it was all my fault. And that's when I first started getting into the bondage modeling, remember?"

Kevin nodded.

"I didn't really give your friend an honest answer when he asked me about that. Remember he asked why I started doing that kind of modeling instead of some other kind? And I told him it was because it was essentially harmless and lots of other girls wouldn't do it and so the money was good? Well, those things were true, I suppose, but they weren't the real—"

Mrs. Hale," broke in Kevin urgently. "I-I mean Mrs. Durning. Please. You don't have to—"

"I think an honest answer would have been that when my father died of that stroke, I felt as though I'd done a horrible, horrible thing to him, and that so long as I remained bound, and chained, and gagged and handcuffed, and locked up in those crazy harnesses, in all those endless photographs of me your friends have collected, there'd be no way on earth I'd ever get free to do a horrible thing like that again— that so long as I was chained up that way, the world would be safe from me." She laughed ruefully. "It was a pretty fair plan, I suppose, for the poor, confused, troubled child I was then. The only problem was that so long as I remained all chained up that way, I couldn't do much of anything. I couldn't live. I wasn't free to enjoy a real life."

Kevin glanced about him, at the grandchildren's drawings magneted to the refrigerator, the bird feeder outside the windowsill, at all the spice jars and utensils and culinary paraphernalia of the warm country kitchen in which they were standing. "You obviously beat it somehow," he said finally. "Got a secret?"

"Forgiveness," she replied quietly. "Forgiveness is the secret. It took me years, but I finally taught myself how to forgive."

"You mean," asked Kevin, "you finally forgave your father for—"

"No," she answered, cutting him off with an impatient shake of her head. "I mean I finally forgave myself for wanting him dead."

CHAPTER 36

▼

PORNO QUEEN IN DE

The funereal tabloid letters screamed at him across the litter-strewn aisle of the subway car, but the infuriating way the Puerto Rican asshole was folding and scrunching his newspaper made it impossible for Kevin to decipher the rest of the headline.

PORNO QUEEN IN DEATH PL

Kevin cast his eyes desperately about the subway car, hoping to locate some different, more compliant rider reading the same paper.

No luck.

He dove off the train at the next stop and looked about frantically for a newsstand. *Nada.* But there was a refuse bin stuffed to the brim with discarded newspapers, and Kevin managed to snatch a virtually unsoiled copy of just the one he wanted from beneath the covetous paw of a bag lady a millisecond before she could get her mitts on it. She gave him a snotty look as he grabbed it, as if proprietary rights to all subway refuse had somehow been conferred upon her.

Kevin's casts were off now, but he was still moving gingerly about with a cane. Now he flew through the pages of his freshly garnered prize, trying—

PREZ'S FLOOD CONTROL PLAN A WASHOUT

Oh Jesus Christ! muttered Kevin under his breath. Where in the fuck—

PORNO QUEEN IN DEATH PLUNGE

A curvaceous blonde porno queen is being listed in critical condition in Bellevue Hospital this afternoon after allegedly attempting to take her own life in a despairing death plunge from the dizzying heights of the Queensboro Bridge.

The apparent intended suicide, clad only in hot pants and halter top, has not yet been identified, but all signs point to her having been a denizen of Manhattan's sleazy sex for.... A pair of bronze tokens, imprinted with the name Pornomart, were found....

Kevin hurled his newspaper back into the refuse bin and hauled himself up the two long flights of stairs to the street. "Bellevue Hospital!" he stammered anxiously to the cabdriver. "And hurry! Please!"

But it was the heart of the evening rush hour, midtown Manhattan was gridlock city, and Kevin knew he would've been better off clenching his cane between his teeth and crawling the eighty or so blocks to Bellevue on his hands and knees.

The place was like a grisly zoo when he got there, because it was always a zoo, one of those venerable New York City health care institutions where unless they've brought you in with multiple gunshot or stab wounds, you might as well give up any hope of ever laying eyes on a doctor.

Kevin elbowed his way to the admissions desk, past mangled but still sentient accident victims, addicts with gaping knife wounds, wives pummeled into unconsciousness by their husbands, and whores savagely blackened and bruised by their pimps. He watched as a tiny infant, hurled out of a sixth-floor window to drive home a telling point in a family quarrel, sped down a white-tiled corridor on a wheeled cart bound for oblivion.

"Excuse me!" he gasped out finally to the bullheaded, walleyed nurse on duty. "The girl in the paper—"

"*Who?!*" she snarled at him, with sullen belligerence.

"The girl in the paper!" blurted Kevin inanely. Oh god, he could see now he should've brought it with him. "PORNO QUEEN IN DEATH PLUNGE?!?" he proclaimed in strangled exasperation, moronically flailing his arms about in a frenzied attempt to hold her attention from the heaving ocean of ambulatory death swirling about them.

And, by god, the stratagem worked, or at least so it appeared. Old bullhead rolled her eyes ceilingward—"Hmm!" she murmured. "Porno queen! Hmm!"—her capacities strained to the fullest by her somnolent effort to access a cranial computer long since wiped clean by hard-disk crash. "Hmm. Yes. Over there. Officer Jamison—the huge one over by that candy machine. See him? He's raising his foot to—"

Kevin whirled round and stood up on tiptoe, peering intently over the throng of bobbing heads in an attempt to home in on the target of Old Walleye's zombie gaze. In a tiny semicircular alcove ringed with vending machines, a whale-girthed plainclothes policeman in sweat-soaked shirtsleeves and shoulder holster, was locked in brutal kung-fu combat with a recalcitrant candy machine, steadying his cyclopean bulk against a quavering radiator pipe as he—

"It wasn't me, Kevie!"

Kevin whirled, like a dervish whirling in an upright grave. She was standing beside him now, and she touched his arm. "It's not me, Kevie. But that's what you must've been worried about, right?"

Kevin's head throbbed wildly, and his heart was exploding, the way those slabs of concrete do when the morons from Con Edison tear up the street.

"It was Trish, Kevie. You remember Trish, right? From the Mart? She streaks her hair this color, just like me." A tear glided smoothly down the slope of her cheek. "I should've watched her closer, Kevie, you know that? Serena—remember Serena, the girl who's psychic? She warned me this was gonna happen, Kevie! She *warned* me!" Pause. "Kevie? You gonna take me out for a cuppa coffee someplace or what?"

They found a Greek coffee shop on Third Avenue and sat in a booth. Her mascara was all streaked from crying, and her clothes were rumpled, as though she'd sat up all night in them. But she had begun to glow, the way women in love do, and Kevin found himself becoming nervous and confused all of a sudden, the way he always did when he couldn't tell whether the glow or his perception of it originated with him or with them.

"... night you kicked me out, it made me so sad and upset, I just wanted to go crazy, Kevin. I just wanted—"

"I didn't kick you out, Vicki. You stormed out. You threw—"

"N-No, you're right, Kevie," she stammered nervously, "technically you're right. But you would have—you would have kicked me out eventually, you know that's true. And besides..."

And she was sad, he couldn't recall ever having seen her so sad before, the combined effect of reliving their breakup and the nearly fatal suicide attempt of her friend. And all at once Kevin could feel himself becoming sexually aroused, and the fact that he was becoming so aroused both bewildered and frightened him, because he couldn't tell whether he was becoming aroused because he loved her and wanted to protect her from the things that made her unhappy, or whether it was because he was some kind of fiend who was getting his rocks off from seeing her so sad.

"... got so stinking, fucking blitzed I couldn't see straight, and you know what I did?"

"No, Vicki. What?"

"I took a penknife, a sharp one—you know, one with one of those sharp little extra blades that nobody uses? And I-I carved ... I carved ..." She was crying unrestrainedly now, sobbing, her blotched black mascara streaming in smeary rivulets down her face. "... your name, Kevie, into my thigh. Only I wasn't so sure if it should end with an 'e' or an 'i'—you know?—so I just left it with an 'i' because I didn't want to fuck it up—you know what I mean?—and so I figured an 'i' would be okay, and if it needed an 'e' I could add it in later."

Kevin didn't know what to say. He wanted desperately to say the right thing, only he didn't know what the right thing was. "You shouldn't have done that, Vicki," he said softly.

"Why not?"

He didn't know why not. He only knew that, crazy as it was, he admired her deeply for having done it.

"Look under the table, Kevin. I want you to see it."

"Vicki. Please. There's no—"

"I know I lied to you about the smack. I don't want you to think I'm lying about this."

"I know you're not lying," he said tenderly. "I don't have to see."

"They stared lovingly at one another across the formica tabletop. He reached out and gently lay his hand on hers.

"I called you a couple of times right after," she said finally, breaking the silence. "I hated you so much at first, and I wanted to at least come collect my stuff. But every time I called, all I ever got was that fucking—"

"I know. The answering machine. It—"

"*Whaat!?*" She jerked her hand roughly away from his and her blue-green eyes sparked with anger. "You *knew!?* You *knew* those were my hang-ups on your answering machine and you didn't even *try* to—"

"Vicki! I-I just couldn't call you then!" Kevin stammered, rushing on, in a desperate torrent of words, to tell her about Guido Gallante, and the collection man who broke his legs, and the hospital.

"You still had plenty of time to call me, Kevin!" she fumed furiously. "You had a fucking shitload of time and you fucking well *know* it! All I wanted to do was make a date to come pick up my stuff, Kevin! You still have a shitload of my fucking clothes, Kevin! My clothes and—and costumes! God, when I remember how I used to dress up for you in those costumes! They cost me a goddam fortune, you know that, Kevin?"

"Vicki! Please! Let's—"

"I swear to christ, Kevin, if you've been letting some other cunt so much as touch my costumes, I swear to fucking god I'll fucking gouge your eyes out!"

1112749

Made in the USA